NIGHT ZOO

Night Zoo

—

Sarah Barr

LENDAL PRESS

First published in 2022 by Lendal Press
Woodend, The Crescent, Scarborough, YO11 2PW
an imprint of Valley Press · lendalpress.com

ISBN 978-1-912436-75-0
Catalogue no. LP0009

A CIP record is available from the British Library.

Cover design by Seline Layla Duzenli and Peter Barnfather
Text design by Peter Barnfather
Edited by Paige Henderson and Seline Layla Duzenli

Printed and bound in Great Britain by
Imprint Digital, Upton Pyne, Exeter

Contents

Heatwave

Hollyhocks and lupins show crisp brown pods, ready to pop. The paint on the white five-bar gate is blistered and smells of paraffin. The yellow lawn scorches her bare toes when she tries to run across so she comes straight back in.

'This heatwave is dangerous,' Dad says. 'Don't play outside.'

'Lie on the couch,' Ma says. 'Lie quietly, Liza,' she gasps, wiping her forehead with the back of her hand, then drawing the shiny green curtains across the window, making a clattering noise. The flies have stopped buzzing and crawl slowly across the deep sill or lie with little feet pointing up. Ma stretches out on the mat by the window as if she's got chickenpox or some other disease. Cholera, like the grown-ups in *The Secret Garden*, which would be terrible. Liza's kid brother, Robert, lolls under the dining room table, unable to push his red metal car anywhere. Baby Clemmy is in her pram in the porch and very quiet today. She's a good baby, Ma says.

Nobody can cook lunch, so a little later Ma creeps round with bowls of mashed bananas which they can barely be bothered to spoon into their mouths. They want orange juice, cold, cold, sour orange juice, but they drank it all yesterday and the shop is shut as it's Sunday, not that it matters because nobody could walk up the hill to the village. Clemmy feeds herself her bottle of milk as she lies back in the shade of the porch.

Hours pass and, boring as it is, Liza can't summon up any enthusiasm to move.

The phone rings, its warble cutting through the sultry afternoon. In the distance, she hears Ma talking, saying things like, 'Isn't it hot and why not leave it till next Sunday…welcome for tea then…we haven't got much to eat today…it's the weather…we could be in the tropics.' There's more muttering as Liza drowses and wishes for ice-cream and delicious freezing strawberries, which she doesn't get.

'Can you believe it?' Ma shrieks, returning to the dining room. 'Some folk can't take a hint.'

Dad lifts his head up off the table, which has paper and envelopes heaped on it, but he hasn't been doing anything at all. Liza has been watching him do nothing. 'What?' he says.

'I'm beginning to wish we'd never had that phone in-stalled,' Ma says. 'It makes it all too easy.'

'It was already here when we came, Martha,' Dad says. Liza can't be bothered to add that the phone is useful for calling the doctor, like when Dad had appendicitis. 'Who was it?' Dad asks.

'Who do you think?' Ma says. 'Cynthia.'

'Oh,' he says. 'It'll be Jack and his usual and I don't think I've got a bean.'

'Shush,' Ma says, looking at Liza. 'Do you have to? I mean it's not as if we're—'

Dad shrugs, gets up slowly, pushing his chair back. 'I feel sorry for them. In that awful, decrepit house.' He plods upstairs and the ceiling above Liza creaks and thuds as he walks around, searching and singing, 'Ain't nothin' but a hound dog,' over and over. She's not sure exactly what he's searching for. If it's that half packet of Rolos, he'll be disappointed because she's eaten them and even if she hadn't they'd have melted to a pool of chocolaty toffee by now. She remembers the argument, Dad saying there were twelve Rolos in the pack and Ma that there were eleven. All because she, Liza, had secretly nicked one.

But she also suspects he's looking for something else. She's watched her father on past Sundays, talking to Jack out in the vegetable garden, encouraging him to grow spinach – 'So delicious and easy to grow from seed' – or carrots because the soil is sandy. Jack nods and smiles, then Liza sees her dad hand him something – it could be a packet of seeds. Before Jack emigrated, he and Dad worked as engineers at the same place. Now, Dad's friend is back in this country, pauper-poor. He, Cynthia and beautiful Susan live in a very old house with a lav that has a trap-door in it to keep out rats, and a green slimy bath.

'Righty-ho,' Dad says, when he returns to the room after a while, puffing a little, and still humming that song. He slips his feet into sandals. 'What time will they arrive?' Her Dad is kind, Liza thinks, although nobody ever says it. She already believes that kindness is one of the most important things, maybe the most important thing, in life.

'About now,' Ma says. 'But she mentioned they might run out of petrol.'

'Put the kettle on,' Dad says, 'Any Swiss roll?'

'Stale,' Ma says. 'We could use the last of the christening cake. Liza, you can't lie there all day, you'll never sleep tonight. Go fetch a bottle of milk from the outhouse, please.'

When Liza gets outside, the sun wallops her in the face. Never look at the sun, they told her when it was the eclipse, so she doesn't, she squints between her fingers. The garden path shimmers in the fierce light, like magic. She glances over to the gate and is surprised to see Susan's family's navy-blue car with its silver front bumper and cracked yellow windows already parked in the lane.

She creeps through the bushes close to the hot, sticky fence, her arms getting scratched by the holly and spider webs sticking to her face. She manages to get near without being seen. The car is shaking and rattling and someone's crying. Is it Susan? Or is it her mummy? If so, what has she done wrong? Susan's dad shouts angrily, she can't hear what but it's something like, 'Why? Why the devil can't you be more careful?'

As she crouches in the centre of the rhody bush, Liza hears the car door open and then sees Susan slide out quietly. Susan tiptoes through the gate and along the path, her long red hair swinging behind her in a ponytail that's tied with a lemon bow to match her lemon frock. She isn't crying but she looks sad. She's taller than Liza even though she's six months younger, but she's no better at playing bandits or explorers, and she's not as good at walking along the top of the high wall. Susan tried it just once, a few wobbly steps, before begging Liza to help her down. If Susan had fallen, she might have cracked her head on a stone and lain white-faced on the grass, legs twisted, like a girl in a story. But that would not have happened because Liza would have caught Susan and saved her.

Susan waits by the side of the house, looking in the front window, her fingers plucking at the rough red brick. While Susan's back is turned, Liza sidles along the back of the bushes then jumps out shouting, 'Hello, Susan, I can see you!' Her friend shudders, a frightened expression on her pale, freckled face.

'Oh! Just waiting for Mummy and Daddy to come, just —'

'Let's climb trees,' Liza says, scraping sweaty hair away from her face. Susan smooths down her dress. It looks like an iced cake. Liza would love it but she's wearing a shrunken faded smock that hasn't looked right on her since she was four.

As they walk away from the house, Liza remembers she never took the milk to the kitchen. They'll think she's forgotten – they say she's 'impractical'. Liza has never told anyone about her memory. Sometimes she wishes she didn't remember word for word what people say, all those sentences arranged so clearly in her head, ready to voice themselves when she'd rather forget.

Liza takes Susan's hand and pulls her up the slope to the shady trees – apple, pear, a big oak and some silver birches. She scrambles into the low fork in the apple tree. 'You climb up and sit here. I'll crawl along the branch,' she explains.

Susan shakes her head, her eyes downcast. She smooths the yellow material as if it's the only thing that matters. 'I can't. You climb, I'll wait. This dress was sent from America and it was very expensive.'

'Take it off, then,' Liza says, 'you must be boiling.' Susan giggles, her pale face going red. 'Sometimes I climb up in my—' Liza stops because she thinks Ma would be cross with her if she tells Susan about how she plays outside in just her knickers and liberty vest when it's washing day.

'In your what?' Susan looks interested.

'My dressing-up clothes. I showed them to you when you came for my birthday, remember,' Liza says.

'Can we do dressing-up now?' Susan asks. But putting on those fox furs and Ma's sweltering velvet cloak is absolutely the last thing Liza wants to do on this hot day.

'Later. Let's go and eat peas,' Liza says. She scrambles along the rough, swaying branch, lowers herself over it, then swings from it back and forth before landing in the grass and rolling over down the slope. Even the moss and tree roots are baking in the sun.

Liza and Susan lie in the long grass at the side of the vegetable patch, a heap of peas between them. They break open the pods and thumb the line of peas into their open mouths. These peas are usually delicious, sweet and cool, but overnight their pods have wrinkled and turned yellow, the peas become floury and slightly bitter. Even so, Liza gobbles them up, and Susan's as well. Liza is just about to run over and grab some more when she hears the men talking as they make their way to their usual spot by the vegetables.

Only yesterday, Dad told her about the 'two-legged birds' that had been stealing his crop so there were never enough peas for a meal. 'Two-legged birds?' Liza asked, thinking which birds have more than two. She tried to imagine a bird that had more. Dad laughed and she wasn't sure if he was joking or not.

She puts her fingers to her lips and the two girls lie down flat in the long grass, trying not to giggle. Ants run along Liza's arms. Susan lies with her eyes shut, little red heat bumps appearing on her neck and face.

Liza remembers when she was younger, looking over the gate at the mad rabbits with bulging eyes running round and round on the grass by the woods. She was standing on the middle bar of the gate with Ma's arm around her. Dad said, 'I need a rifle, put them out of their misery.'

Ma said, 'Can we still eat rabbit, with that disease?'

Dad said, 'Only if well-cooked.'

Liza imagined Dad shooting the rabbits, the banging, the squealing, the blood. The scene lodged inside her head as if he'd actually done it, which she's pretty sure he hadn't. Now she has a horror of rabbit stew. They try to kid her that the meat is something else – chicken or mushrooms – so she is always suspicious of anything in a sauce.

Dad and Susan's dad amble over to the rows of wilting spinach. Liza peeps up and sees Dad is carrying a shopping bag. Liza scrunches her hair away from her ears to hear better but even so, it's all mumbles. Dad offers Susan's dad a cigarette and smoke curls up above their heads - she can smell it. Dad shakes his head, mutters, 'I don't know, Jack…is it such a good idea…'

Susan's dad's voice is higher and more shouty. 'I can manage one. Just one. Two is too many. You know that! You see the fix we're in.'

Susan is asleep, her mouth hanging open, making little snores and snuffles. Liza feels like going to sleep herself, now the sun is going down, the day not so sweltering.

'Money won't do it!' Susan's dad yelps, wiping his face with a hanky. 'Don't know where to go, who to ask. Do you? Can you help us?' Dad shakes his head slowly which surprises Liza. Dad always knows who to ask if they need something. The two men walk to just a few feet from where the girls are flat out behind a ridge in the long grass.

'You could try this,' Dad says, taking out of the shopping bag the green striped cardboard shoe-box that once contained his leather work shoes and which, as Liza knows only too well, has been kept hidden at the back of the wardrobe ever since they moved here. 'Martha suggested a douche…but she didn't like to say.'

Doosh is a nice-sounding word that Liza hasn't heard before. She will remember to write it in her notebook.

Susan's dad takes off the box lid and peers inside. 'We decided against using it,' Dad says, his voice wobbling as if he's embarrassed or very tired. 'We just couldn't.' Dad couldn't? Liza is puzzled and yearns to understand.

'I realise that,' Susan's dad says, sniggering.

Inside the box is a funny brown rubber thing with a squeezy pouch attached to a tube. Liza knows this because she's got it out of the box a few times then hidden it back in the wardrobe. It was like something Dad would use to clear the taps or drain, something that water goes through and you squirt, she thinks, but she's never asked because she knows Ma's and Dad's bedroom is private and she shouldn't be ferreting around in there.

'I'll take it. I'll make her use it. Make her,' Susan's dad says, putting the box back in the shopping bag which Dad fills up with spinach and beetroots he yanks out of the parched earth.

'It may not work at this stage,' Dad says, catching hold of his friend's arm. 'And it's risky, be careful.' Susan's dad just goes, 'OK, OK.'

Liza imagines it must be something useful for their old-fashioned, stinky bathroom. She doesn't tell Susan what happened while she was asleep, but later she goes over and over it in her head: the vegetable plot, the two men, what was said, until the scene fixes inside her.

That night there's a thunderstorm, the rumbling and bellowing coming nearer, then giving tremendous cracks right above their house. Liza lies in bed watching her bedroom lit up in an instant, a huge shadow of her rocking horse against one wall, then all dark again.

Dad comes in. 'Are you all right, sweetheart?' He goes over to the window and shuts it. Liza runs out of bed to stand with him and look through the wet glass at the fruit trees shaking their branches in the lightning and the gate banging to and fro at the side of the house. 'These curtains are soaking,' Dad says, drawing them over the window. 'Jump back in bed. I'll check on Robert and Clemmy.'

Liza hears and watches the storm all night. In the morning, the house is still and cool. The grass outside is wet and fresh on her bare feet as she runs across to pick peas in the vegetable patch.

House of Spirits

'You can't go out like that, Anna. I can see everything through that Aertex shirt – put a vest on.' My mother's words and her disapproving stare made my cheeks flush, my chest tighten, ashamed of my eleven-year-old body.

I ran upstairs, pausing for a second in front of the long mirror on the landing. It was true. Two pink lumps had appeared on my chest. That was bad, obviously. I tore off the revealing white shirt and rummaged in the moth-bally drawer, finding an old vest which I squeezed myself into. I was fat. I pulled on a home-knitted, thick jumper that would scratch my skin and give me spots.

'What on earth do you want to walk that dog for?' she said, laying out biscuits on a doily-covered plate. They were crisp biscuits with hard, glossy, coffee icing and I knew the ladies' flower-arranging class would eat the lot.

I hesitated, scuffing the edge of the green kitchen lino with my sandal, unsure whether to tell her I wanted to be a vet like Katherine (very unlikely as I wasn't clever enough). Or, say I felt sorry for Mr Pearson, on his own as

Mrs Pearson was out at her job. I said nothing.

'Go on then, they'll be here soon.' She wanted me out of the way before her friends arrived. I wasn't what a girl should be, probably not what she'd been like. 'And don't go into Mr Pearson's house. Stay outside if he gives you a drink. Remember what I've said, now.'

I raced down our tarmacked drive, jumping high, higher, kicking my heels, pretending to be the funny, bucking Shetland pony at the riding stables. I loved animals but I wasn't much good with them, was even a little frightened of them. I didn't know why I'd set myself the challenge of walking an enormous Labrador which was bigger and heavier than I was. Once a day for the whole summer, that's what I'd agreed.

The Pearsons' house had originally been identical to ours. But theirs had peeling paint, long dry grass for lawn, a pot-holed drive and a ramshackle carport where we had a garage.

They couldn't afford to keep it up. My parents said Mr Pearson wasted money on things he shouldn't, especially considering he was retired.

Tawny heard me coming and bounded down the path, a massive yellow monster who had no respect. He jumped up, his smelly, dripping tongue wrapping itself around my face, hands, toes in open sandals. His claws tugged loops of wool out of my jumper.

'Come on, you terror.' Mr Pearson walked out onto what he called the verandah, and fastened a lead on the straining hound, waved goodbye and off we went, tearing out into the road, the lane, the dusty, summer woods.

I had a choice, be yanked wherever, or let him off the lead, watch him disappear into the scrub, then spend an hour calling, calling, before returning, usually on my own. If that happened, I'd loiter in the lane outside our houses, waiting for Tawny to turn up, looking pleased with himself and covered in cow-pats.

This afternoon, keeping him leashed, I eventually managed to pull him to heel at the edge of the woods. Although I felt drawn to the gnarled, lichen-dappled trees, clay pits, and bogs that could suck you down, it was a place I wasn't allowed to go into on my own. One day I would, fearless like Mr Pearson in the Himalayas.

We went back up the hill. We met an Alsatian. Predictably, Tawny yelped, snarled, and charged over the road. The horrible Alsatian leapt at me, its teeth ripping a hole in my sleeve. Its owner grabbed it.

'Keep control of your dog and stop it pestering mine!' he bellowed.

I tied Tawny to a lamp post and went into the corner shop. The man tutted but he took the pound note and the written instructions and handed over the brown parcel, which I had to carry carefully back. I checked the time. I could return – the hour was almost up.

This was the sort of thing my mother totally disapproved of. I knew that, eventually, someone would tell her that I was being sent on errands by 'that man', who didn't want to be seen going into the village stores because word would get back to his wife. But for now, we were getting away with it.

Mr Pearson was in the garden, smoking, with Chotapeg, their little terrier who was too ill to go walkies.

'How are you, Annabella, Mirabella? Goodness, you must be boiling in that woolly. It's the middle of summer my girl, didn't you realise? Come in and have a glass of something.'

'Is Katherine at home?'

She was the Pearsons' only daughter, cool as a cucumber, and at University. 'Smoking pot is far less harmful than smoking ordinary cigarettes or drinking to excess,' she'd said, shocking my parents who'd invited them all round at Christmas. When the guests had gone, Mum and Dad had a big argument. It was something about – why did we have to live on this sort of a road?

'No, Kate's in Marrakesh. You look as if you could do with an ice-cream soda and I could manage something, too.' We went inside. He poured a tall glass of lemonade, dolloped two delicious scoops of vanilla ice-cream into it and finished it off with a handful of raspberries, a multi-coloured straw and two wafers. 'Now, how do you like that?' I liked it very much.

'What do you think of this, just come out?' He put a record on his player and, with a shaking hand, he placed the needle. 'We all live in a yellow submarine, a yellow submarine, a yellow submarine—'

'I didn't get it, now I'm enjoying it, undemanding. Lord knows what it really means. It's Kate's. What do you make of it?' he asked.

'It sounds happy,' I said.

'Happy. Yes. Happy. Hippy.' He sighed and then laughed.

He took the parcel I gave him and unscrewed the bottle of vodka. After he'd poured some into a tumbler, he filled the bottle with water and pushed it right to the back of the kitchen cupboard. 'Don't tell Mrs Pearson. She thinks I don't know she knows and I think… well it's complicated.'

'Here's to my old friend Barney.' He gulped the drink. 'That's good, Bella. Poor man, he got mauled by a tiger, up in the hills.' Mr Pearson liked remembering about when they'd lived in India. 'Life was hard but exciting,' he said. 'Then they made me give up the farm and come back here to put my feet up.'

We sat in the conservatory. He rummaged around and found a bottle of what he called malt. He poured himself a drink then wrapped the bottle in a blanket and squashed it back into the window seat. 'Here's to my cousin, Tony, who distinguished himself in the war, an exceptionally brave fellow. Dead.'

He kept brandy in a wellington boot and would sample that next.

'When you get to my age, all your friends are dead.' I felt sad and he must have noticed. 'Correction. Not all my friends,' he said, 'because I've got you to play chess with.'

I patted the two dogs, both now docile in the sun. We set out the chess pieces on the teak board Mr Pearson's father had made. The pinnacle of pleasure for me was simply looking at those pieces, ebony one end, pale woody colour the other, all lined up in exactly the same order each time we started a game. I loved the symmetry. I liked noticing the differences between the ornately carved kings and queens, and the tiny plain pawns, so unassuming but which, if luck was on their side, if they played their game cunningly, could become queens.

I knew the moves. We started to play our customary game. Mr Pearson almost always won, but that was OK. I didn't expect to win. Just occasionally, his concentration lapsed and then he'd accept his downfall with good grace. 'Mulligatawny soup, I've left the rook undefended!' I looked out for signs that he was letting me win deliberately, but I didn't see any.

This was why I put myself through the whole dog-walking torment, although I never admitted to anyone that it could upset me.

'Here's to you,' he said, raising his glass as I took his castle. 'You're clever. And good at keeping secrets.' I nodded, trying not to smile too broadly at these compliments. 'You could be a detective when you grow up. Or how about a spy? The world's your chess-board, Annabella, Mirabella. Remember that. The world's your chessboard. Plan your moves, wait for your time. Don't give up.'

The Gold Watch

It was nearly closing time on a cold January evening when the gentleman came into Messrs Featherstone and Cotton, clanging the door to and stamping mud off his feet.

'Go and see to him, Jenny,' Mr Cotton said through a mouthful of pins. He was in the storeroom, arranging hats on stands ready for the following Monday. I was sewing Petersham ribbon around a felt beret. I wasn't a trained milliner but could adapt and prettify the hats my employer bought in.

My job was long hours for low pay but it made all the difference for me, Mam and the three little ones. To the outside world, it was a respectable job, even though all sorts came into the shop.

Unaccompanied gentleman customers rarely knew much about hats. If they did come in to choose one as a present for a lady-friend, it would usually be returned the next day. Sometimes the woman asked for the money back, which was awkward.

This man wore a homburg, a military-style overcoat and

he was carrying a newspaper. He had the solid, sleek air of the wealthy.

He wanted a broad-brimmed lady's hat – 'frothy' he said. He meant muslin and lace. I explained that, as it was winter, we had that style only in black. Not many women want to be swathed in black lace, unless they've suffered a bereavement, of course. I didn't say that, though. It was too close to home for most people, with the war and then the grippe.

The customer smirked, picked an ostrich feather from the pewter jar and tickled my chin. He took out a gold pocket watch. 'I've got an appointment the other side of town in one hour's time. Be a good little girl and find me a hat. Fashionable but not one of those turbans.'

As I passed him with the step-ladder, he squeezed my bottom, and when I yelped, he twizzled me round close to him, pushed away the steps and kissed my mouth. His lips were soft and his tongue tasted of whisky and tobacco. His stubbly moustache was sharp and stinging against my nose. I sneezed.

'Shush,' he warned, pulling away suddenly and pinching my nose.

'I'm not that sort of girl, sir,' I said, pushing roughly at his plump, waist-coated chest. I knew to nip this sort of attention in the bud. I wanted to make something of my life.

'Are you not?' he whispered. 'Then don't tempt me with those big brown eyes.' He watched carefully as I climbed the steps. I was all too conscious of the darned holes in my black wool stockings. I lifted down a tower of hat-boxes. 'Chop-chop, the hat, please, missy.'

Mr Cotton was clattering around in the back, packing things away. He went to his sister's for dinner on Saturdays and wanted to leave on time. I'd go and fetch him if there was any more nonsense from this customer. I could always ring the bell, which was close to hand.

I was shuddering inside but wouldn't allow this to show. I kept wiping my clammy hands across my skirt, hidden by the counter, while the gentleman looked through the choices. At least he didn't ask me to try any on.

He chose a coffee lace hat left over from autumn stock. I packed it in a cream and brown striped hat box which he strung over his arm. 'My offices are in this part of town,' he said as Mr Cotton came in to take the money. As I opened the door to show him out, he murmured in my ear, 'Beautiful, soft hair.'

I noticed he'd left his newspaper behind but I didn't feel like running after him, so I folded it and popped it in my basket to read on the bus on the way home.

'Your cheeks are very red, Jenny. Not sickening for anything, I hope,' Mr Cotton said. He was a funny old bloke, a self-made man, set in his ways but not unpleasant. He had a horror of illness so first thing every day he drank a pot of boiled-up smelly herbs.

I was like the daughter he'd never had and, when he thought I looked despondent, he would bring me small boxes of chocolates. He was older than my father would have been. I started to explain what had happened with the customer but I felt embarrassed. Mr Archibald Cotton was from that generation who divided women into categories and I didn't want him to see me as the wrong sort. He might give my job to one of the other young hopefuls who regularly crept in, pretending at first to be customers but who probably couldn't afford knickers, let alone a hat.

'A bit forward, sir, that's all.'

'He paid in cash, Jenny, and we've got the spring collection arriving next month. He'll be interested in that.' Mr Cotton looked at me quizzically over the top of his horn-rimmed spectacles. When I'd started at the shop, I was a child straight from school, clumsy and slapdash. Now, he was reaping the investment he'd made in training me.

I did a quick brush around the shop floor - too late to get down on my hands and knees to sweep up pins and ribbons that had rolled under the counter. I'd do that on Monday. I put on my coat and the bottle-green cloche hat, my pride and joy, even though it had a faded side from being in the window too long, and struggled out against the wind to catch the number seventy-three omnibus home.

First, I treated myself to a bag of hot chestnuts from the brazier by the bus stop, cracking them open once I got seated, protecting my hands with my gloves. Half were rotten, but the rest were floury and sweet. Apart from the last customer, it hadn't been a bad week.

'Daisy, Daisy, give me your answer, do. I'm half-crazy all for the love of you. Daisy, Daisy…answer do…half-crazy…love of you…Daisy…' Someone on the bus was humming the tune, making the words go round and round in my head, sounding like a barrel organ.

The song made me think of my intended, George. How he said he wanted to marry me. Dear Georgie with his long skinny legs, shiny carrot-coloured hair and memory for useless information. It would take years to get that nest egg together so we could set up home. No chance of us living as a couple with either of our families, we were all squashed in like sardines in a tin. Tomorrow afternoon, all being well, I'd see George. He'd bring round his new bicycle to show me and, although it was hardly the weather for riding out, maybe we'd take a spin round the park, me on Mam's old bone-shaker, as she wouldn't be using it on Sunday.

'It won't be a stylish marriage, I can't afford a carriage, but you'll look sweet upon the seat of a bicycle made for two, a bicycle...a bicycle made for...'

I doubted whether Mr Cotton would keep me on in my job once I'd married, despite the investment he'd made in me. Me not having a job would be a problem. George and I would be mouse-poor. But happy and in love, I reminded myself.

The bus conductor tapped me on the shoulder. I paid my fare and then opened the *Evening Standard*. A small headline caught my glance: 'Artist's Lover Plunges to Death'. It was sandwiched between a notice for 'Lectures in Philosophy and Psychoanalysis' and a Selfridges & Co. advertisement asking for more lady store assistants.

I'd never heard of the artist, Modigliani, or his common-law wife, but it seemed such a heart-wrenching story. She'd thrown herself out of a high window, demented after the death of her lover. Twenty-one, just one year older than me. She'd been expecting a child.

What it must be to love to that extent. Would I do the same for George? Would he for me?

I'd ask him tomorrow, it would be a test for him, but I could already hear his reply. 'What d'you want to go upsetting yourself for with that nonsense, Jen? Them sort of folk, they live different lives from us.'

'Yes, but they have the same feelings, don't they George?'

'I'm not sure they do, Jen,' he'd reply.

I imagined that distraught woman standing on the window sill on a grey, January day and looking down on a busy Paris street, way, way below, freezing as she hurtled down towards the horses, carriages, trams and shoppers. Couldn't anyone have saved her? Or was she in disgrace with her family for never marrying so better to be dead?

I read the section above this report: 'Lectures will take place in the Great Hall Every Week at University College, London and visiting speakers will include Dr Sigmund Freud, Dr Gregor Simpkin, Dr Bertrand Russell and Miss Anna Freud. Topics to be covered, amongst others: The Interpretation of Dreams; The Child's Imagination; The Nature of Reality; a Preliminary Hearing of Dr Sigmund Freud's new commentary on 'Delusions and Dreams'. All welcome, Fee: One Guinea for Ten Lectures.'

I would love to go to those lectures, but a guinea, I couldn't afford that in a month of Sundays.

I longed to know more about dreams, what those everyday items such as an umbrella, hat, watch or tramcar really signified in the kaleidoscope of my dreams. There was so much more to life than our mundane routines, though I wasn't one for spiritualism and séances, which were a fashion amongst some women now so many of us had lost loved ones. George had been unable to fight, thank God, because of his weak eyesight.

But biology, mathematics and the workings of the mind, I longed to discover more. I had borrowed everything available at the Boots lending library, which wasn't a great deal. How could I get to those lectures? These thoughts took over from thinking about the deaths of the artist and his mistress.

'Upon the seat of a bicycle made for two…But you'll look sweet…'

George was mad about cycling and I liked it, too. Freedom, the wind in my face, no customers to please. I could forget about Mam having to take in washing, darning and ironing to make ends meet. About my not being able to go to college as Dad had promised.

When I got home, Mam was in a dreadful state. Lily had a high temperature and could hardly talk, her throat was so sore.

'Can you see any spots on her, Jen?' Mam asked fretfully. She'd sent Harry round for the doctor, which would be another expense.

'She looks rather blue,' I replied. We were aware of the tell-tale signs of the disease that had spread fiercely and with no warning from the trenches. Those dark red spots, the lavender-coloured skin and the rasping breathing which meant the flu infection had lodged in the lungs. 'But I think it's just a bad cold.'

We wanted to forget the way the illness had carried Father away. Apart from the agony of watching him slip into unconsciousness in such a short space of time, his departure meant we toppled from our secure way of life to one where we were forever on the brink of destitution.

I took out my week's wages and handed the majority over to my mother.

'I didn't go to the butcher's, Jen, so we've got enough for the doctor.'

We made up a bed of cushions for Lily in the scullery, then Mam, myself and the two boys sat down for a scratch supper. We had just finished washing the dishes when there was a rap at the door. 'Dr Brownley! Hurry! Wipe the table. Put some coal on the fire,' Mam commanded.

But it wasn't the doctor, it was Mr Cotton. He'd never called at our house before and I was amazed he'd managed to find his way so far east. He stood upright and clearly ill at ease just inside the front door.

'Sir, is everything all right? Your sister…?'

'My sister is well thank you, Jenny.'

Mam gave a little bob of her head. 'Would you like to

speak to my daughter on her own, sir?'

We went into the front room but he wouldn't sit down. 'Jenny, this is a serious matter.'

I wondered what on earth he'd come about and, for a moment, I thought he was going to ask if I would – but, no. He looked grave, angry even.

'I've had a complaint.'

'About me, sir?'

'Yes, Jenny. It seems that the last customer who called into the shop mislaid a valuable gold pocket watch.'

'I saw him look at his watch soon after he came in through the door,' I said.

'I rather wish you hadn't said that, Jenny.' He paused. 'I had rather hoped the gentleman was mistaken. That he'd never brought the time-piece into Messrs Featherstone and Cotton.'

'I didn't take it, Mr Cotton, I hope you don't think I did.'

'I didn't say that, Jenny. However, the gentleman, a Mr Ravenscroft, claims it was stolen.'

There was a long pause during which he jingled some coins in his pockets and paced the few steps across the room, then the few steps back.

'I believe you to be an honest girl. But we can all be tempted.'

'No sir, definitely not.' I was indignant. How could I prove my innocence? The customer's word against mine and I knew who'd be believed.

'This Ravenscroft fellow says he rested the watch on his copy of the *Evening Standard*. And these items got covered by all the hats so that he forgot them. I told him I never saw a newspaper on the counter. Did you, Jenny?'

'Well, yes sir. I, I…it was only an old newspaper.'

'Oh dear.' He knew I liked reading on the way home.

'But, sir, did you really search the shop? Did you look through that pile of paperwork on the side table, and under the baize in the window?'

'Yes, Jenny.'

According to Mr Cotton, Mr Ravenscroft would be calling at the shop at nine o'clock sharp. He had said that if I returned the watch, which was a valuable heirloom and also of sentimental value, he would not call the police.'

When Dr Brownley arrived we were a very subdued family.

'Don't worry so much,' he said to my mother. 'Worry is bad. Your daughter's a strong girl. Her chest is clear and she just has a head cold. Steaming with Friar's Balsam should help.'

When the others had gone to bed my mother said to me, 'What are we going to do, Jenny? It will be difficult, if not impossible, for you to get another job without a good reference.'

'I think Mr Cotton will keep me on,' I replied, though I doubted it. The rumours would spread round that area of town and ladies who didn't have enough to occupy their minds would shun the shop for amusement.

Mam didn't question my honesty, and I was comforted by that. Neither did George who was highly indignant when he heard the story. I toned down the details about the customer's physical assault. We didn't go for a bicycle ride due to the cold wind. Instead, we took a stroll around the park.

'I don't remember the customer putting his watch down on the newspaper, George.'

'He probably didn't. Just trying to blame you for something that's the work of a pickpocket.'

'But what shall I say?'

'Stick to your guns. You didn't steal it and they can't prove otherwise. Did he ever actually own a proper gold watch?' He was trying to encourage me but we both knew whose side the police would be on. 'Whatever happens, we'll manage, Jenny.'

Some children were skipping on the sodden grass, watched by their nanny. '*I had a little bird, its name was Enza. I opened the window and in-flu-enza. I had a little bird...I opened the window...*'

That poor Modigliani woman had jumped, not flown, from an open window.

'She was a criminal, Jenny – suicide and murder – don't feel sorry for her.'

'Do you really believe that, George?'

'It's the law, Jenny, in this country anyhow.'

'Some laws are wrong.'

'Maybe, but people like us can't change them. You don't even have a vote.' His thin, freckled face and blue eyes were very dear to me and as he kissed me goodbye, my stomach churned at the unfairness of the choices available to us.

I lay awake from four a.m. on Monday and could not manage to eat my breakfast. I was at work by seven-thirty. I searched through every single hatbox. I smoothed out every sheet of scrunched-up tissue paper.

Mr Ravenscroft arrived at nine, unaccompanied. Mr Cotton brought him into the shop, which was not yet open to the public, and questioned him about what had happened. I listened, looking down at the counter. I didn't trust myself to look the customer in the eyes as anger was seething within me.

'Well, Jenny, is there anything you'd like to say?' Mr Cotton asked, in a not unkindly tone.

'I never touched the watch, Sir. I'm sorry, of course, for

the gentleman's loss.'

'You wouldn't want to have to go to the police station, would you?' Mr Ravenscroft said.

'Was it a very valuable watch, sir?'

'Very valuable, indeed. It had a special mechanism. It only needed winding twice a week, and was bequeathed to me by my late father.' He smiled showing stained teeth with gold fillings. His eyes were cold and unsmiling.

I wondered if I should offer to make recompense, a few pence a week until it was paid for. But that would make me look guilty.

'You're a pretty girl, Jenny, a very pretty girl, and a nice one, I'm sure. This is a very unfortunate circumstance.' He paused and stared at the tears which I couldn't prevent springing from my eyes. 'Mr Cotton has told me he can't afford to employ someone with a police record.'

'Come on, Jenny, I'm sure we can clear up this misunderstanding,' Mr Cotton said. His face had a crumpled, blotchy look. 'I'd like to keep you on, but—'

'I'll leave you to consider things,' Mr Ravenscroft said.

As I opened the door for him, he clamped his heavy hand on top of my trembling one. 'Come round to my office by noon with or without the watch and I won't take the matter further. Mr Cotton says you're a clever girl. I may have a position to offer you, with prospects.'

As he went through the door, he turned back, pushed his face close up to mine and quietly hissed, 'You could have silk stockings, throw out those ragged wool ones.'

He had made the whole incident up, I was sure of it now, and was relishing his power over me. He was an evil man and I couldn't see any way out.

When he'd gone I sat down in the corner behind the counter and got my frock all dusty as I sobbed.

'Dear, dear, what are we to do, Jenny? He's such a very influential man,' Mr Cotton said. 'I'll make a pot of tea before we open.' He disappeared into the backroom.

The blank faces of the hat-stands stared down at me from every direction. I kicked my toes against the cupboard below the counter. It was time I slid the feather duster underneath to clean out all the oddments that had rolled there.

As I bent down, pushing the feather duster vigorously around, I noticed a gleam of gold amongst the dust. I leaned farther forward and picked it up. It was attached to a chain and the chain was attached to a…watch. I pulled it out from underneath the cupboard along with scraps of fabric, tangled threads, pins and buttons. There it was in all its importance, a very valuable gold pocket watch. It was not large, the case was attractively engraved and it had a solid feel. The numbers were Roman, the time was correct and the watch was ticking in a self-confident way. It must have rolled off the newspaper, unnoticed in the hustle and bustle of unpacking hats from boxes.

I could rush straight round with it to Mr Ravenscroft's office, that would be the best thing. But how guilty I'd look, even so, returning it so soon after his visit.

I suspected that returning the watch wouldn't give me much protection against tittle-tattle or my employer against loss of business.

While I thought about what best to do, I slipped the watch back under the cupboard, well out of view. I would retrieve it just before closing time. I wondered if it really was as valuable as that man claimed. What a difference the watch could make to my life, and my family's.

Mr Cotton came in with a tray of tea. 'I had a sleepless night worrying about all this. But in the light of day, and having had the meeting with the gentleman, it doesn't seem too bad. He can't prove anything, and frankly, the police have more important things to do. These so-called suffragettes are still up to their antics. Now, that is something to worry about.'

He had surprising strength, Mr Cotton, and I respected him greatly for supporting me.

'Thank you very much, sir.'

Maybe I wouldn't lose my job. But even if I did, with the watch I wouldn't be penniless. And Mam wouldn't have to worry about doctors' bills.

'As for going round on your own to see that fellow, you simply mustn't. I'll accompany you.'

I had to wrestle with my conscience. But all things considered, I didn't feel I was doing wrong. Not if you thought of what some people did.

I would go to a completely new area of London with the watch, take it to a jeweller's or, failing that, the pawnbrokers. How much could I raise? Whatever the amount, I'd divide it. Half to Mam who'd then likely have a year without money worries; half to me and George. Enough for us to rent, for a year, a perfectly respectable villa with its own front door. A villa by the sea would be perfect. Peaceful, with healthy air.

When closing time came, I couldn't bring myself to retrieve the watch. I wanted to think about it overnight, so I left it hidden in the dust.

The next morning, Mr Cotton greeted me, with the watch in one hand and a bunch of snowdrops for me, in the other. 'How on earth did we not find it yesterday?' he sighed happily, tugging his silk cravat into place. 'I always knew you were an honest girl, Jenny. When I return from seeing the Ravenscroft man, of course there's no need for you to see him again, there's something of a personal nature I'd like to ask you…'

My relief was only partial. Marriage, if that was what he was offering, wouldn't be in either of our interests, and I could not let it happen.

The watch was returned, but, according to Mr Cotton, its owner seemed surprisingly disappointed to receive it.

At lunchtime, we each had a bowl of soup. When he started to speak of the personal issue, I interrupted him. 'Mr Cotton, I am grateful to you for everything. You've taught me so much and are like a father to me.' I felt myself blushing but had to continue. 'I'm sorry, I'm not sure what you want to ask me but – I think it's best I go. I should start looking for another job.'

Now that the watch trouble was cleared up, I could apply for the Selfridges job I'd seen advertised in the newspaper.

'I quite understand,' he said, a little sadly. 'I'll give you a good reference because, Jenny, you are quite exceptional especially for one so young. Without you, though, I may have to retire.' He didn't offer me his shop and I didn't really expect it. There were so many reasons why he wouldn't even have considered it. I was so young. But it was one of my dreams to run a business and there was still time for that. He was happy for me to stay on until I found a new position, which was a relief as I couldn't do without an income.

So I boarded the number seventy-three in lighter spirits. Lily's health was improving. I was confident I'd find another job. George might one day gain a promotion. The days were lengthening and the chestnut trees were beginning to bud. I hadn't stolen the watch.

The East Room

'It's freezing, Franny,' Doug says. He's wearing old ripped jeans. Our favourite Leonard Cohen is playing. 'Wasn't Dad going to run central heating up here?'

I'm sitting at the folding card table in my fleece and bobble-hat, plus fingerless gloves so I can work on my laptop. 'It's Scotland. I like being cold.'

'You do not!' He laughs and for a second I imagine he's going to run over and tickle my ribs like he used to when we were younger, before he changed and became wary. 'Nobody likes being cold.'

'An open fire makes me cough.' Has he only just realised the East Room is unheated?

'Electric heater - I'll find you one.'

He knows perfectly well most electricity is made from fossil fuels. 'I'd accept a wood burner but—' I grin over at him as he lounges on the sagging horsehair sofa. Above us, roof-lights frame the pale January sky and chalk clouds. We're in the attic of the Old Manse where I've lived since I was nine. 'What I really want is solar panels. For the whole house. That'd be perfect!' I can feel my cheeks reddening. As if I think solar panels are the most important thing in the world!

'Listed building,' he says. 'Spoiling the roof. Dad's not going to allow that.'

I tell Dougie I'm making a list of points on 'The Impact of Scottish Independence on the Environment' and he's interrupting my thought flow. I say it jokingly because I don't actually want him to go away. I type: *Renewable energy forms: Wind + wave power (exploit Scotland's resources); solar; geothermal.*

'Come to Singapore,' he says. 'You'll not be cold, I promise.'

Is he serious? Nobody would let me do that. 'And do what?'

'Duh! For a holiday, not to live. You're going to uni.'

'If I get that far.' All those years at private school and I haven't got a place at St Andrews or Oxbridge. Nobody has criticised me or said I've wasted their money and the opportunities they offered me. It's embarrassing.

'Fran, you'll sail through, get a good degree. Then a fantastic job, one that makes a difference. To the world.'

'Like you, you mean?' I'm totally torn about Singapore. If I went there with him, I could convert him, make him revert to his passionate environmental roots, I know I could.

'Don't get into all that.'

'Banking. Who would've believed it?' I sound petulant. Why can't I be sophisticated? He got me into this environmental stuff then sold out. I still like him, though. *Like.* It's too weak a word to encompass my feelings. But I never let myself dwell on how I feel about him, never put it into words, even to myself.

There are so many weak words in life, words that need definition. Nice. Good. Fair. Family.

'You'll have to get a haircut before you go, dear Coz,' I say, as if we're in a Jane Austen drama, and also to remind us about our relationship.

'And you—' he stands, stretches his arms high. He can touch the ceiling up here. 'Need to pack your bag.'

'I know he can't bear me hanging around, but I've not decided whether I'll go.' Uncle wants me out of the way. He's got someone in mind for Doug. Someone who'll strengthen the (already healthy) family finances – and not weaken the gene pool. He's always been unreasonably suspicious about me and Dougie.

'You're going,' Doug says, and his mouth sets in a firm line. Does he want to be rid of me, too? 'Mum will miss you. But you want to see your folk. Especially your brother.'

Is he jealous of Will?

Aunty only likes me because I read *Hello* magazine to her and tell her funny stories.

I'm feeling disillusioned with this overprivileged family but don't want to quarrel with Doug.

'See you,' I say, and we give each other a bear hug. He tugs my plait gently. I lean into him and he warms me.

He touches the fine gold chain around my neck and lifts up the enamelled butterfly. 'Did I give you this?'

'Have you forgotten?' I see from his serious, grey eyes that he hasn't forgotten. 'Fairly traded gold,' he said then, on my sixteenth birthday, and I trusted him. Still do.

'Define 'fairly-traded',' I say.

When he's gone, I pack my worldly possessions into a rucksack and canvas holdall, ready for the journey south.

The last time I made this journey was six years ago and everything was a blur. Berwick-upon-Tweed, Newcastle, York. 'You're going home, it's not your home, you're going home, it's not…' the train chunters. I've drunk my latte and now I'm eating marmite sarnies. Home. Define that word, that idea. Is it where I was born? Is it where my family are? Who are my family? Is it where I feel safe, most natural?

I'm wearing my favourite vintage outfit – it was Aunty Mary's. Apparently she was wearing it when she met Uncle at the Café Royale. They're bringing back these Laura Ashley prints but this is the real thing.

'We are not paupers, Frances,' Uncle said, his Scottish accent emphasising every vowel. That word, 'paupers', it's hurtful, patronising. 'You've no need ta' wear old clothes.'

He doesn't get it. I'm not going to buy any clothes at all, not even knickers, for one whole year. I'll never ever purchase anything made by slave labour. Those poor people who died in the fire in Bangladesh. Why would anyone go on wearing clothes made through murder? My other environmental pledges are: no flying, no meat or fish, no out-of-season fruit and vegetables and no antibacterial soap that kills dolphins.

I make my way by tube to Paddington and the next train. I could save a great deal of money if I went by coach, but the train's more environmentally sound.

I'm going home, I'm going home…

Despite my pledges, I end up having to take the bus for part of the journey because of floods and a washed away track. The thought of global warming swims in my head, a global warning.

Mum's sister had money. A big house. She wanted a daughter. They said I'd receive a first-class education, which I wouldn't get at home. They said Mum was ill, neglecting herself and her kids.

I was proud I'd been chosen. But then I had to set off with my cardboard suitcase. Will took me to London, bought me a *Little Princess* comic for the journey. Aunty's friend collected me at Kings Cross. I remember crying, leaning against the window, misting it up, and her telling me off. 'You should be grateful – you're a lucky little girl,' the friend who never smiled said. Why didn't I run away from her when we reached Edinburgh, get on the train straight back home? Then again, I was only nine.

Homesick doesn't begin to describe how I felt when I started my new life in Scotland. I couldn't understand these people with their weird accent and they couldn't understand me. Then somehow I got used to them.

Mum sent a card and present every birthday and Christmas. I went back for two weeks each summer until I was thirteen when I made my feelings known. I was angry she was keeping Susie and the boys close to her but I'd been chucked out as if there was something wrong with me. 'You wanted to be rid of me!' I screamed.

'We wanted the best for you!' they replied. But there was no space for me in their lives. I'd become the bolshy teenager who refused to have anything to do with them.

I tore up the stupid cards that arrived with 'To My Darling Daughter' emblazoned on the front and smelling of sickly violets. Aunty said, just send them a postcard, or a text now and then, keep in touch, they're not bad people. No way. The next summer, I refused to go back to see them.

That's sad, forgetting my own family, and now I feel guilty.

It makes me feel sick, looking round the carriage and seeing all these take-away cups and packets. It's a plastic society. Live the life you want to change. Or is it, change the life you want to live? When we stop, I'll collect up the litter for recycling.

At Plymouth bus station, I look around for Will or Mum even though I know they haven't said they'll meet me. I walk around and wonder if I should buy presents but I don't know what they'd like. I don't have enough money to buy for all of them. Would Mum want flowers? Or is it weird to turn up with a bunch of carnations, as if I'm a stranger?

Where is my mum when I need her?

I buy a box of chocolates then take a bus to Stoke.

The terraced house is smaller than I remember. There's a scattering of snowdrops in the front garden.

'Dear little Franny, at last! At last!' Mum cries when she opens the door. Her hair's gone grey. She kisses me several times, takes the chocolates but says she's on a diet. We go along a narrow hall and into the kitchen. 'It's an extension,' she explains. 'It was dark and poky, remember? But this opens it out, don't you think? It's all gone on the mortgage, we'll never pay it off. Cupboards from Ikea. We got rid of those pine ones, and chose these – painted! What do you think of the colour?'

I say I like the colour. I think it's bound to feel awkward to be here. I've got used to space and light, big windows. She hands me a mug of tea and looks at the box of chocolates. 'Not a make I've heard of,' she says, picking up the toddler clinging to her legs. 'This is darling Maisie, such a sweetheart, say hello to Frances.' Maisie turns her head away and Mum jiggles her.

'They use fairly-traded ingredients. Sugar, cocoa—'

'But do they taste good?' she asks.

My two younger brothers burst into the kitchen from the living room, kicking each other, then rolling on the floor 'Mum, he took my—'

'Mum, he stopped me watching my—'

'You promised I could choose!'

When they notice me, they stare in a way that would be rude if they weren't kids. 'Say hello to your big sis,' Mum says.

They snigger hello, point and shout: 'Granny Franny, Granny Franny!'

'It's your dress,' Mum explains. 'And the cape. Scottish?'

I want to run away and hide. 'I'll take my things upstairs.'

'I asked Susie to clear her room up for you, but you know what she's like. Did I tell you Will's been posted abroad? You'll be sorry not to see him.'

I can't bear to ask which war zone he's gone to this time.

Susie's bedroom is cluttered with clothes and make-up flung around. There's a folding bed in the corner.

'I've told her to give up her bed,' Mum says, 'but, looking at you, you could fit on the put-you-up.'

I go back to the kitchen. The boys shout complaints. 'That's horrible! Bag of rubbish! Mum said you had gifts for us!'

'What's this, Franny?' Mum asks. 'You never ate all these sandwiches, did you? All these crisp bags!'

'Just recycling. I'll pop it in your bin,' I say, feeling bad that I haven't brought presents for the kids.

Susie returns and isn't pleased to see me. She tidies her room and puts away the New Look tops and leggings. 'Help yourself, it's all cheap stuff. You don't seem to have the right gear,' she says, rubbing gel through her hair and spiking it. 'It's the twenty-first century in Devon.'

Dinner is beef stew. Feeling sick, I nibble some forkfuls. Susie says they are having lessons at school about eating disorders and how it's about mental problems, not just wanting to be thin like models. There's a silence in which Dad stares at Mum.

'So Fran, what went wrong? Why didn't you get into college after all that private education?' Dad says.

'I'm on my gap year, doing an environmental project,' I say. 'I'll carry on with it here, on my laptop.' The boys snigger.

'Pay well?'

'It's voluntary.' I want to call him 'Dad' but the word won't come out.

It's clear he doesn't think much of my decision. He's older and quieter than I remember. He's still in the fishing industry but now he says it's day trips for tourists, not the real fishing he used to do, hauling in big catches in all seasons.

'You can't be my sister,' Susie says when we're in bed with the light off. 'Why didn't you come back to see us? You didn't even come when Gran died.'

I try to explain how I was very young, I didn't want to go, and how I felt lonely and cut off from them.

'Don't whinge. You're the lucky one,' she says. 'Living like a princess. Not having to cope with Mum's moods.'

It's March and I'm walking along The Hoe on my own when I receive a text: *M lonely. D put solar panels on barn. East Room bored without u. Come home? Doug x*

Without hesitating, I decide. My absence has changed things – they feel differently about me –and I feel differently about them.

A letter arrives from Uncle inviting Susie to come too, for the Easter holidays, and for longer, if it works out. I try to talk to Susie about the invitation, explain what might be in store for her, but she doesn't hesitate to say yes.

The day we leave, I unclip my butterfly pendant. 'Borrow it for the journey, and for luck,' I say, handing it to Susie.

I imagine she's nervous. But when we say goodbye to everyone, she's unfazed. The boys are already moving their stuff into her room.

Mum hugs me and whispers, 'Don't think too badly of us. You have a better life up North. Susie's a handful but they will help her as well.'

We travel by bus, then take the east coast train. She gazes out of the window, a happy smile on her oval face. She's wearing an angora jumper and skinny black trousers. Something good has come out of my visit to Plymouth. She's clever and she'll have opportunities, education.

'Soon be home,' I say as we take a taxi at Edinburgh Waverley. When I say the word, 'home', it sticks in my throat, then comes out in a whisper, then echoes around my head, like a song. Is here home? It seems disloyal to think or say so, and I don't feel sure. If Scotland is home, then Plymouth can't be. But I don't truly belong in either place and I don't know if the not-belonging matters. Susie doesn't notice my struggle, or if she does, she politely ignores it. Politeness is something she's developing fast.

We have dinner and Susie pleases everyone by relishing her meal and expressing delight with everything, including the venison which she's never eaten before. Uncle relaxes and I can almost hear him thinking it's not going to be so bad, having another niece to live with them.

Doug, Susie and I go into the East Room. 'It's a little warmer in here,' Doug says, shivering. 'But not what I'm used to now.'

'The cold peps me up, gets my brain going,' I say, looking at Susie sitting on the old sofa, pulling her sweater sleeves over her hands.

'You always were an eccentric creature,' he says.

'I'm a warm-blooded creature. I envy you in Hong Kong,' Susie says, giggling.

'Singapore,' Doug says.

She blushes and fiddles with the butterfly. 'Never was good at geography.'

Dougie notices the pendant, glances at me, then back at her in the white sweater. I realise she's pretty, as well as determined.

'I'd love to travel,' she says, 'when I've finished school.'

'Not bothered about air miles then?' he asks and she replies, no, she's never thought about it.

Doug's expression softens and he says, 'Let's see if Fran has some music you'd like to listen to, Susie.' He puts his arm around her and they go over to my pile of CDs to choose a song. I feel a wrench in my heart. I'm angry with Susie, and worried for her. What have I let her into?

I'd like to rewind six months and start again. But as that's not possible, I console myself with the thought that, for a few days, Doug will be here with me in this place I can almost call home.

Stopping by Woods

The woods are lovely in this pink winter light, the setting sun glinting off snow and the bare branches like a Japanese painting. I needed to come back, to remember, to feel the ground beneath my feet.

I padded downstairs, heard cooking sounds, clicked the door behind me, pushed open the garden gate. Now I'm in my wilderness. It's just as it ever was: strange and healing.

I'm running, slipping past the trees, catching their smooth and knobbled bark with my hands, scuffing the fallen leaves, crisp with frost, jumping over branches that look like discarded limbs. I remember smelling moss and bluebells in spring, bracken in summer, mould and fungus in autumn.

Too much safety is oppressive. I could never bear being cooped up with Mum and Dad in our perfect home. I started by escaping into the woods where I could breathe, then, later, to the other side of the world.

Mum pleaded with me, her precious only child. 'Promise me you won't go into those woods. It's dangerous, Helen. You don't know who you'll meet.'

There is a way that curves and divides but which, if you know it, leads to the centre, to the fallen oak tree. 'Not when it's dark. Not on my own,' I lied.

'They say someone fell in the bog and sank without trace.'

'I'll be careful,' I said.

I felt scared, but relished the danger. I was by turns sleuth, spy, escaped prisoner, French Resistance fighter, camou-flaged during the day, a shadow at night.

Being on my own was something I treasured. I wanted to free myself from my parents and their hopes. It was peaceful in the woods, especially in winter. I could sit and watch the changing shapes, the occasional bird or squirrel, a spider spinning its web.

So when Ricky turned up, I was angry.

I heard him before I saw him. Making a weird shrieking noise like a trapped wild creature, bellowing like somebody who knows no one will help him. Pulling at branches and letting them slap back, pushing through brambles, rip-ping his clothes.

'Shut up! Stop that racket.'

I reach the crumbling fallen tree now, sit down, pull my coat closer around me. It is icy tonight. I'm on my own – silence, shadows.

'This is my place,' I said, pretending I hadn't noticed his blotchy face. He was standing in front of me, staring distractedly. 'Which way did you come in?'

He waved his arm behind, to where I knew there were farm cottages. 'It's my place. I found the tree first,' he argued, not giving in, despite the tears clogging his throat.

He was a boy who got on the bus and kept out of the way, but he had a determination about him. He was in the year below me at school.

In the months that followed, sitting with our backs against the tree, we drank our first bottle of whisky, smoked our first joint, followed by many others, cut our fingers with the potato-peeling knife, exchanged blood. We listened to each other, and, I suppose, learned to share our place. We didn't have sex, but we carved our initials on the tree.

'Best mates forever,' I said at the end of the summer term.

'Yeah, right. When you're a doctor or a city lawyer, and I'm herding cows. Doesn't seem likely, does it?' he said. He was thin, dressed in skimpy clothes too short for his limbs, and that summer evening he had bruises on his arms and a cut lip. Even so, he was a nice-looking boy.

'Our friendship is more important than money,' I said, too naïve at seventeen to realise how offensive that was to someone who had none. Who needed to escape more urgently than I did.

'You don't know how lucky you are,' he replied.

I invited him back to my place and Mum treated him like the son she'd never had.

He didn't invite me back to his. His stepdad was unpredictable and his mother was too busy with her other kids.

'Promise me you won't go on your own,' Mum said when I bought my Europe travel card.

'Going with Ricky and Julie,' I said. But Ricky had to earn his keep over the summer on the farm, and Julie and I fell out as soon as we got to France. It was better that Mum and Dad didn't know any of this.

When I got back after four weeks of bumming around, he'd gone, their cottage boarded up.

Back at school, someone said he'd passed his exams but his parents wouldn't let him stay on. There was a row with a teacher on results day; his stepdad lashed out – he'd been drinking. His mum took the three boys and went to some women's refuge up North.

'Where?' I asked. 'Where have they gone?' No one knew. No one told. It was safer that way.

I kept trying to find him.

I did go to Uni but didn't have a settled career, preferring jobs here and there, around the world, keeping in touch but always with a good reason why I couldn't come home.

But now I have. I walk to the other side of the woods, see the modern estate which has replaced the farm, think of Ricky.

My mobile clicks – a message now I'm out of the wood. Then it rings. 'Helen, where are you?' Mum's anxious voice crackles from the phone.

'Just getting a breath of air,' I reply. I'm here for a few days because, of course, we need to see each other, but it's hard to break the old patterns.

'Don't stay out on your own,' she whispers. 'Dad's ready to carve.'

Taking the quick way back by road, I listen to Ricky's message again. His familiar voice reminds me how he's found a flat for us. He trusts I haven't changed my mind.

He's the lawyer, not me. He likes his life to be organised and safe, which I understand now.

I think about the tiny shifts and changes that keep the woods a living, breathing place. I think about the paths criss-crossing it; different ways, many choices. I phone Ricky as I walk alongside the edge of the dark woods, say everything is fine, say I'm sure we'll be together soon.

On the Platform

I'm looking at my watch again. The bright, cold sunlight slanting onto the tracks and over the platform confirms it's still morning, a Friday morning in March. Something happened to the Eurostar after it reached this side of the Channel, some incident, so hundreds of travellers were forced to find other routes. Many of them crowded into this branch station along with me on my journey home. I let the previous train go by. I'm not in a hurry. Don't want to stand squashed up against armpits and rucksacks. The next train is delayed. On top of everything else that's going wrong today, I have a heavy period.

The girl on the bench next to me is cradling a bundle. She's maybe fourteen or fifteen with a heart-shaped face and long dark hair. She's patting and rubbing the tiny baby's back, trying to soothe it. The baby's cries mingle with the gulls' squawks as they circle overhead, watching for discarded crusts. The girl pulls a dummy out of her bag but her baby won't be pacified. The platform is crowded with people hunched into their scarves and coats, hands

wrapped around takeaway drinks. A few taxis pull up outside – I can see them through the wire fence – ready for
those whose determination cracks. The side gate to the
platform has been opened so a crowd can escape quickly
and safely.

How come the girl has a baby when she's just a kid
herself and has no idea how to look after it? She probably
doesn't even want it. As soon as I think this, I try to pretend
I didn't mean it. But it's difficult to dismiss a thought that
keeps pushing its way back into your mind. Who am I to
judge whether she's a good mother or not? I'm having a
horrible day and I'm feeling sorry for myself. I never, ever
want to do this particular journey again. My stomach cramps
sickeningly. I hunch over on the bench, try not to groan.

The girl glances at two men standing a few metres away,
nearer the platform edge, crammed against a woman with
a bike, an old man with a huge suitcase and a couple each
carrying a child. The girl's unfashionable clothes, the baby's
grubby shawl and the screams mean she won't attract ad-
miring attention from anyone, least of all from those two
guys, one of whom is wearing an expensive-looking leather
jacket. She's now looking at them from underneath her
curtain of hair, perhaps hoping for money. But she's wasting her time. Men like that never give to beggars, if that's
what she is.

She's just a kid herself and should be with her own mother, but her mother's likely to be slaving away to make ends
meet, or off her head on something.

I'd like to help the girl, but if I do it could get very
complicated. Perhaps she doesn't need help. She looks as
if she's had enough of waiting. She's getting to her feet.
The leather jacket guy turns around and mouths something
at her – something rude, from his expression. Is it the

baby's screams he objects to or has he noticed the teenager looking at him? He mutters angrily to his companion. The girl sits down. There isn't much room to move.

I shift nearer to her. 'Ignore them. They're not angry with you. Or your baby. It's the waiting. Everyone's edgy.'

She nods seriously, as if trying to understand me. She rocks her hiccupping baby to and fro.

My mobile rings and against my better judgement, I answer.

'What a bummer. You gave everything to that fucking department, Marie.' His voice is distant.

'Yeah, I did, I did. How did you find out?'

'If you want any help, anything I can do?'

I would love some help, his help, but I know his words are hollow. Even so, even though over a year's gone by, and even though he's a shit, I still want to hear his voice. I hesitate, thinking of ways to keep him talking. 'No, there's nothing but...' My stomach clenches and blood trickles down my legs, inside my tights.

'Was there a row? Did you, you know, break the rules, like the time—?'

'It's a bit of a story—' I say. Where do I start?

'Wanted you to be the first to know. Our news—' he says.

'What?' I press the mobile into my ear and hear the dreaded words. One click and he's gone. 'Love you,' I murmur pointlessly and without really meaning it. 'Once did.' The loss of my job's going to be bad enough but the loss of hope is worse.

The girl touches my arm lightly. 'Here, lady—' I can't place her accent. '*Bambino*.'

'What? What do you mean?' I say.

'*Disperato*.' Or is it 'disappeared? I'm not sure. She points to the sign for toilets above the waiting room door. 'You take. I go. Please.' She picks up the baby's pink dummy which has fallen on the floor. It's dusty and no way would I use it.

'The next train is high-speed and will not stop. Stand away from the platform edge,' comes a message over the tannoy.

'You don't know me,' I reply. 'You can't hand your baby to a stranger.' I've no intention of getting involved. But the pleading expression in her green eyes and the baby's intoxicating smell – milk, cotton, skin – I can't help getting closer. The sucking sound the baby's making, her lips going in and out, her eyelids fluttering, her face peaceful, sleeping, as if crying never happened. I relent. I understand she doesn't want to take her baby into the toilets as they aren't the cleanest.

'*Minutos*,' she says, holding up three fingers.

I force my tired face into a smile. I also need to go to the toilets urgently but when I arrived on the platform, there'd been a long queue and it put me off. The queue has now gone. She hesitates, looks at me searchingly as if deciding whether she really can trust me or not, and then she thrusts the baby into my arms. I wrap the blanket more firmly around this featherweight and nestle her inside my wool coat, careful not to let her face rub against it.

The girl slips away quietly, ducking and weaving past people along the platform, through the waiting-room door and presumably to the ladies. Leather jacket man turns just as she disappears and searches for her with his eyes. Does he know her? She needs to be quick because the train will soon be here. Or will it? Does anyone have any idea when the next stopping train will arrive?

The elderly man with enormous suitcase shuffles backward surprisingly quickly and lands on the bench in the girl's place. He pulls a newspaper out of his anorak. The headlines declare: 'Security Increased at Airports!' 'Refugees Starving!'

When we get on the train, I'll go with the girl and sit near her, in case she gets herself into something she shouldn't with those two men. The smaller one, wearing a cap, is scrolling down his mobile. The taller guy in the leather jacket is jiggling impatiently from foot to foot.

'The train now approaching is high-speed...Stand away from the platform edge. The train approaching platform two is the through train to...and will not stop.' People try to move back from the platform edge. But it's impossible to move, everyone's wedged. The baby snuffles and squirms and is going to start crying again any moment. Where is the girl? I glance back to the waiting room door, see her emerge and push, hunched down, into the crowd. She's hidden, and all I notice are the annoyed faces of the couple she must have barged into. In the distance, the train screeches through the tunnel.

I suddenly think she's going to hurl herself onto the platform edge, and over it. She's that desperate. I stand up and scream 'Train! Girl! Save her!'

The old man next to me grunts, 'Sit down. You're scaring your baby.' Apart from this, nobody hears or cares. The train rockets past.

Leather Jacket and his sidekick stare pointedly at me and move in my direction so I tuck the baby back into my coat. They are shoving people aside impatiently, angrily, but making slow progress. Now they're gazing beyond me and I realise they're not that interested in me – they're looking towards the fence and the gate. It must be about the girl. They must know her. I don't think they wish her well.

I crane round, and suddenly catch sight of her slipping through the open exit. She's followed by a mass of people all heading out of the station to the taxis. The two guys are trapped in the middle of this morass. The girl disappears and, of course, I've no idea where she's gone. She's maybe got into a taxi if she has the money, and if she's managed to avoid her pursuers, or darted between the cars and across the patch of green to the bus station where there will be many buses lined up to take her almost anywhere if she's quick. I'm jubilant – she's escaped! But from what? What about her baby? She wouldn't have forgotten the baby.

She's made a choice.

I don't hesitate. I grab my workbag and hobble as fast as possible, given the crowd and my churning stomach, in the opposite direction to the main flow of people, over the railway bridge, keeping low down to avoid being spotted, and towards the shopping centre on the other side of the station. The baby is snug in my coat.

Seahorse

As we near the station, there are huge posters of seaside things – a fossil, a boat, an ice cream in a cone. Mary's asleep so I can't show her. We get off the train and I push her in the buggy towards the sea. I'm waiting until I can collect the keys.

We've come to this seaside town because it's where someone has offered me a job over the phone without even seeing me, and there's a nursery place available.

Beyond the road is a stretch of wintry grass, beyond that, muddy sand and pebbles scattered with bladderwrack, sea lettuce, kelp, polystyrene cups, syringes and salty rope. I trudge up and down, pulling the buggy behind me. I like counting and naming seaweed and looking for shells. I like the sea – swimming is one of my pluses. I like collecting special things. I look at my watch again – nearly time.

If I could find one precious thing on this deserted beach – a seahorse, for example – I would count myself lucky. Not that I believe in luck. It's just molecules randomly colliding. I don't think a seahorse could live on the beach as it needs deep water. Seahorse is hippocampus, which is also the name of that part of the brain where memories are made and stored. I've memorised the times of high and low tides for the whole of March. I like storing facts.

The sun comes out, so I wear my sunnies, as well as my brown coat, when I go into the rental office to collect the keys. The agent wants references and I explain they will follow, although I don't yet know how. I guess he doesn't have people lining up to rent this particular two-bedroom bungalow. He takes my bank notes and hands over the keys without looking at me. 'Thank you,' I say, putting them carefully into my zipped pocket.

He glances at Mary in her buggy. 'Boy or girl?' he asks. I don't answer unnecessary questions. Then he explains how to drive to the property. I try to show I'm listening and don't tell him I'm taking the bus. It doesn't sound far so I'll probably walk. I pick up my rucksack and bags and march out before he engages me in conversation. Once that's over, I push Mary to the loos behind the arcades. In front of the mirror, I wriggle out of my skirt, cardigan, shirt and shoes and step into dingy old jeans, a man's sweater decorated in snowflakes – it's acrylic so not scratchy –and trainers, all bought this morning from the hospice shop. I put my sunnies back on and tuck my long hair into my newly-acquired baseball cap. These are the first clothes I've bought entirely on my own as almost always Mum or Freya come clothes shopping with me. I don't think I've chosen too badly. I fold up my smarter clothes, then shake them out and chuck them in the bin. I bend over to kiss Mary. It's important she feels loved. I do love her. I love her funny little face and the way she yawns with her tongue sticking out. It's just her and me now so I've got to do everything I can to make her feel right.

Yesterday, there was a partial eclipse of the sun, not that I saw it because of all the clouds. But I knew it was there – a sign from nature.

It's a struggle to open the bungalow door. The key's wonky and needs to be wobbled and turned from side to side until at last it works. While I'm doing this, a woman with a tartan shopping trolley walks up the path. 'Can I help?' She looks at Mary all sleepy and floppy. 'Aren't babies marvellous?' she says in a sing-songy voice. 'They just fit in with life.' I wish she'd go away. She looks around as if expecting to see someone else. 'Is she yours, dear?' she asks, smiling. I know what she's thinking. 'Let me know if you need anything. I'm Doris, next door.' I nod, understanding she wants to be friendly. She points to her bungalow, which is similar to ours, but with more plants in front, coloured glass panels around the door, and a satellite dish poking out at the side.

I walk in and unpack Mary's fleece sleeping bag, bottles, vests and nappies, toucan mobile, and 'Hungry Caterpillar' cloth book. I say, 'This is home,' to us both. If I say things a certain number of times, they become true. When she's had her bottle, I put her covers in a wooden drawer which I've pulled out from the chest and onto the bedroom carpet away from the draught, and then I tuck her in to sleep. I hang my coat and t-shirts in the fake regency wardrobe, slot the *Breaking Bad* DVD into my laptop and turn the sound up. Even so, I can hear the waves moaning on the beach.

'Kelda. Where r u + Mary? Mum gone bananas + wants to call police.' I delete and switch my mobile off. I don't have to answer. Freya's very emotional. I told them many times. I said, I know I made a mistake – I thought he loved me – but I am an adult. Don't treat me like a child.

I grab my rucksack and run into the bathroom. I pull

scissors out and tug my hair straight and chop at it, keep chopping, chopping until it's almost all gone. I was going to dye it but it's easier to cut it off.

The bungalow feels damp but that's because it's by the sea. I've never lived on the coast before but I've always wanted to. It must be because of my fishy ancestors. I stack cans of saver tomatoes and beans and a net of potatoes in the kitchen cupboard. I remind myself about all my good qualities. That's something my teacher, Mrs Armitage, used to do when I was at school long ago. My good qualities are that I like my own company, I can swim well, and I'm practical and have an exceptional memory. But each good thing can be turned around and made a bad thing. I'm too shy and have only had one boyfriend. When I start swimming I don't want to stop which annoys people. I'm too fussy and have to do everything perfectly which takes a long time. I remember too much. Some things I'd rather forget keep crowding in and I have to shout at them.

There's a tap at the door. I flatten myself against the wall and peer out through the gap between the net curtains and the glass. It's my neighbour, Doris, holding a tin. I don't like cake or anything sugary. She knocks again and calls out, 'If you need help, please come round.' She leaves the tin on the doorstep.

Next morning's Sunday. I discover six chocolate brownies in the tin. Sniffing their sharp, gooey smell reminds me of baking with Mum and how I liked stirring and pouring but not eating. I hope the cooker here works as I can't afford takeaways. Mary sleeps through till late. It's the sea breezes. I give her a bottle then wrap her up snugly. Luckily, I have my cap as there are bare patches where I can see my skull, very white, as if I've got something wrong with me. No one will call me Kelda Carrot now.

We wander from one end of the seafront to the other, past beach-huts, nobody brewing tea today, past the café where I will work tomorrow, right to the end under the yellow cliffs. I don't think those houses perched up high, on the edge, will be there long. I don't understand why people aren't doing more to stop the impending global warming disaster. It makes me very anxious. I try to push the idea out of my brain but it's better to do something as ideas in my brain are very persistent. I collect strips of seaweed to hang up to inform me about the weather. Dad told us about this long ago when we were all on holiday in Cornwall. The best holiday ever, Freya said as we drove home singing along to, 'I am sailing, I am sailing'. We didn't know Dad would die. I don't think Mum knew. She changed after that, which isn't surprising. I rip the seaweed off the buggy handles and chuck it at two grey seagulls scavenging among tarry pebbles.

I'm still searching for treasure. A seahorse on the beach would be dead, Kelda, which you wouldn't like, I say. You want a live one. The male, not the female, carries the eggs in his stomach. Seahorses are unusual in nature. A seahorse couple stays together forever, or if not forever, for years. I like it that they're different from the norm, and beautiful little creatures, all bobbly and curly. When I find one it will be a sign that everything will be OK for Mary and me.

When we get back, I put Mary in her pink fleece sleepsuit, and she curls up and over my shoulder like a seahorse. Oh Mary, you are why I left Mum and Freya. I couldn't help it. Now here we are, the two of us, by the sea, and tonight it's cold and spooky and you don't want to sleep. I make you a bottle and cuddle you for hours, listening to you breathing and whimpering.

To begin with, the idea of you was shocking. I couldn't

believe I'd have a baby before Freya who's older and married. And then you arrived with your sleepy eyes and your tiny fingers with soft, peeling nails. I went to parenting classes to learn how to look after you. 'Everything's fine,' I said a certain number of times and then it became fine. But Freya said it was ironic that I'd had a baby accidentally when they'd been trying for years. I realised she wanted to take you away and have you for her own. I realised that's what Freya and Mum were thinking and they were keeping it from me. Mum said, 'You can go back to college now, Kelda. Freya and I will look after Mary.' I knew their thoughts and I didn't trust them. I was crying inside. I would do anything to stop them from taking you from me.

It's Monday, eight a.m., and I'm getting ready to start my new job. First, I sort out Mary, then quickly eat bread and beans and drink black coffee. I'm looking through the window, watching the surf in the distance when I notice a man by our gate, waving at someone. Me, perhaps. Embarrassed, I squat down out of sight. There's a grinding noise. It's dustbin day. He's waiting to take our rubbish and, of course, we don't have any. I run out to explain.

The door slams behind me but the key's in my pocket. I turn, wobble, shake and shove it, but can't make the door open. Mary's safe in her buggy which she can't tip over but I must get back in. The dustbin men drive away. I have to get back to Mary. I run round looking for an open window although sure there aren't any as last night Mum's voice was in my head. 'Lock up safe, girls, and don't answer the door.' Like she used to when we were little and she worked nights.

Two days here and I've messed up. There's a baby shut away on her own. I am a stupid carrot head now. I pull open the letterbox but can't see her, although I can hear hiccupping.

'Let me know if you need anything,' my neighbour said. I go straight over and ring her doorbell. Wait. Then ring, ring, ring.

'It's very early, dear,' she says, opening the door and frowning. Then she realises it's an emergency. 'I've still got the key from when my old neighbour was alive. Nobody thought to ask for it back,' she says. Her key works easily and Mary's fine but screaming her head off, her face red as a lobster.

'Please, come into the warm for a few minutes,' Doris says, 'I can see you're both upset.' So I follow her back into her home, understanding she wants to be neighbourly. Mary kicks her legs on the lounge carpet. Doris pours me tea from an old-fashioned teapot. 'That's my husband's collection, or was,' she says, as I glance at the grey stones lined up on the mantelpiece. 'The ammonites are best, don't you think?'

'Ammonites are good,' I say. I pick up a stone inlaid with a thin curved shape. Its tiny horse-head, big eye and long nose have lain like this for thousands and thousands of years. 'But I like this one best.' It is dead, but it died naturally, not through pollution or fishing nets.

'Then I'd like you to have it. One less thing for me to worry about.' Doris folds bubble wrap around the fossil seahorse and hands it to me. I thank her and then set off to nursery with Mary.

Carpe Diem

The sun beat down through the windows and roof of the Nissen Hut in which Shirley was sitting. Just two girls and Mr Williams in a small room together. Shirley never did the homework and thank God she would never have to make up another excuse.

'I hope over the summer you won't forget everything you've learned,' he said, leaning on the teacher's desk and running his fingers through his hair. 'You've both worked hard. Made good progress.'

Her friend, clever Theresa, grinned while doodling a bespectacled face with a haystack of hair on the cover of her exercise book.

'I hope you'll both remember your Latin teacher,' he said, almost pleading. 'Call in any time you're passing the school.'

'Going to party tonight?' Shirley scribbled on her book and pushed it towards Theresa as he turned his back to rub chalk writing off the blackboard.

Theresa shook her head and doodled a sad face.

Having dropped her duffle bag, emptying its contents

over the floor, Shirley spent the rest of the session collecting these things up. Mr Williams (call me, Chris – and they certainly hadn't) wore a frayed tweed jacket and square black-framed glasses. Cool, or completely drippy? The bell rang and the two girls went out, imagining that he was standing at the window gazing at them. If they'd been younger, they'd have giggled, but they were both eighteen.

'Did you see his wife that time he crashed his car?' Theresa asked as they walked to the library.

'I don't know anything about him.' Shirley had started Latin late after she'd discovered she needed a smattering for her university English course. Mr Williams had scooped her up enthusiastically. Hardly anyone studied dead languages at this grammar school and if the aversion continued, he'd soon be out of a job. Theresa was going to Oxford to read Classics. Shirley was wondering what to wear to the party. She loved clothes but had very few.

'She came to take him home – he was very upset,' Theresa said. 'How old do you think he is?'

'Hard to tell,' Shirley replied. 'Not young. Forty?'

'I thought twenty-nine,' Theresa said, 'same age as my oldest brother.'

'Sure you can't come tonight?' Shirley asked. Theresa's parents were strict Polish Catholics.

'They might have let me if I'd finished exams,' she said, 'like lucky you.'

As Shirley pushed her bike out of the school gates, someone told her that the party had been cancelled. The owners of the derelict building had been warned about an invasion of teenagers and had wrapped barbed wire around it.

Over the summer, she worked at the soap and cosmetics counter in Boots and was surprised to find she liked the job – the mindlessness, the routine, and the space to create fictional lives for the customers. Theresa went to Poland to help her grandparents on their farm. Shirley had not been lucky with boyfriends. Boys thought her odd. She was easily bored. When she got to university it would be different. She would meet someone. That was her hope.

She'd agreed with her parents that she'd become a teacher once she graduated, but she was secretly confident she'd find something better to do. Graduation was three years away!

They needed reassuring that she'd be employed after an education they saw as an indulgence for a girl. Of course, they took a different attitude to her younger brothers. If they'd not had sons, perhaps they'd have seen things differently. Shirley wished she had a sister – their combined voices would have been stronger, more able to argue.

At the beginning of September, she sent her trunk of possessions on ahead by rail. Nobody came to the station to see her off but just as she was leaving the house, her mother gave her a carrier bag containing a few things. When Shirley had settled into the dusty, overheated carriage of the London train, she discovered a green velvet dress which had always hung in her mother's wardrobe, a pink cat and a bottle of homemade lemonade. She had butterflies in her stomach as she looked out of the window, interested in everything she saw, the future stretching ahead, a cool, sparkling river.

When she arrived at the hall of residence, she was surprised to find other girls had their parents in tow, parents who wanted to check the accommodation and settle them in.

She unpacked her trunk in the large room which had two single beds, a patterned rug, and a tiny wrought-iron balcony overlooking the garden. The bathroom along the corridor was shared with others. She hung up her clothes including the hand-me-down velvet dress. It was lovely with long, fluted sleeves and she wished she'd seen her mother wearing it. She felt a sharp pang for her parents whom she hadn't treated that well recently.

She tried to talk to her roommate, Maggie, a geology student who seemed shy, shaking her dark hair and jangling brass hoop earrings in reply to Shirley's questions.

'Do you like this song?' a skinny boy in grey jumper and very clean jeans asked as they stood in the students' union bar. Elvis's seductive voice was overdone and the lyrics naff but 'It's now or never' chimed with her. She tried to give an opinion but the boy wasn't listening. He pulled her towards him, whispering that he loved her short pink skirt and her bare legs, and led her onto the dance floor.

The speakers blared, 'I can't get no satisfaction,' next and after that they threw themselves, gasping, onto a couple of chairs. She smiled at him, crossed her legs and tapped her toes nonchalantly. It was a couple of weeks into term and she was optimistic.

That was how things began with Oliver and she hoped their relationship would develop, although where could they go? They were each in a single-sex hall of residence. At the end of the evening, they agreed to meet again.

She waited ten days for this to happen. Was something wrong with her? What had she said or done? Was she very ugly? They were studying different subjects, so she'd have to search for him and she wasn't going to do that. She saw him in the distance but he never looked towards her. He was too serious for her, she decided, no fun. She tried to stop thinking about him. She read *Paradise Lost* for an essay.

'You could find someone else, not tie yourself down,' Maggie said, as they sat on their beds painting their nails. Maggie stretched out her hands, displaying shiny, dark nails that matched her maroon feather boa. She said she was going to spend the day in the library, and Shirley said she would too, but found herself wandering around the park in the autumn sunshine, feeling homesick. She thought she saw Maggie on the other side of the lake by trees, maybe they were weeping willows, her mother would know, with a man in a bedraggled sheepskin coat.

Then one afternoon Ollie appeared in the library, said he'd been busy studying and travelling home to see his sick mother. He sat down near Shirley and she pretended to read as he studied. She watched him adding and crossing off tasks on a list.

It was annoying that he returned home every other weekend to his mother with her mystery illness.

In early December, they went to the cinema. When they emerged from *Dr Zhivago* to a dark sky lit by flashing neon signs, she wanted to discuss what they'd seen, the tangled relationships, the hopelessness, glamour and romance of these lives. She especially wanted to discuss their own relationship.

The film thrilled her because it told her that she had to seize happiness when and where she could, not waste time. '*Carpe diem*,' as Mr Williams would say. She could hear his voice: '*Carpe diem quam minimum credula postero*.' She longed for a snowy landscape. It was raining and they hurried away from the tube and into a student pub.

Ollie sat hunched over a pint of beer, 'Hate these depressing stories. Hopeless characters who keep making the wrong decisions.' Shirley could see Naomi, another student, on the other side of the bar snogging a boy she'd met in the park. She leaned closer into Ollie.

'I think Maggie, my roommate, is away on a field trip,' she said, fingers crossed that she was right about this, or that if Maggie wasn't trekking around remote geological sites, she would be at an all-night party. 'So you're welcome to come back.' If they unlocked the front door very quietly, took off their shoes, they could creep upstairs to her room without the warden intercepting them. She'd probably be preoccupied, anyway, with the postgraduate student with whom she was having an affair.

Shirley caught hold of Oliver's arm. 'It'll be fine, it's a good time.' She planned to make an appointment, wearing an engagement ring, at the family planning clinic next week. Like all her girlfriends, she was terrified of getting pregnant.

'I'm catching the early coach tomorrow,' he said.

What had gone wrong with the evening?

'I'll be back Monday, so can we meet then?' he said, appeasingly.

She shrugged angrily, imagining the empty weekend ahead.

She had the room to herself that night which was a wasted opportunity. Maggie had left a note that she was going to a jazz night with friends and staying over. 'Come with me next time?' She signed off with a kiss. Mags was nice. Shirley felt lucky, having heard horror stories of room-sharing between new students randomly placed together. But she and Maggie didn't spend much time together, each preoccupied with their search for a man.

She woke to the sound of ducks quacking on the grass outside. Then she realised it wasn't ducks but someone banging on her door and calling, 'Shirley! Quick! Phone for you!' The girl came into the room and watched as Shirley scrambled out of bed, grabbing her cardigan.

'He'll be cut off by now,' the girl said.

Shirley hoped it was Ollie to tell her he'd missed the coach. Hooray! All forgiven. She leaped downstairs. It was only 8.45 for God's sake. The phone was in a cubicle by the front door. The hall was wood-panelled with old portraits in gilt frames.

'Hello!' she breathed into the Bakelite receiver.

She listened to a man's voice. The voice was saying, he was up in town for some convention about something or other, and wondered if she'd meet him for lunch and a chat.

'Who is it?' she asked.

'It's Chris!' he said. 'Don't you recognise my voice?'

'Chris?' she echoed, stupidly. Did he imagine he was speaking to someone different, a girl he actually knew?

'Christopher Williams. Latin lessons, or have you forgotten me already?'

Mr Williams. Weird. But it was Saturday and she had nothing to do apart from writing an essay, and that could wait.

'Tell me about yourself,' Mr Williams said over spaghetti bolognese followed eventually by lemon cheesecake. It was a small restaurant in a side street near the British Museum. Shirley hated this sort of open-ended question that tempted her to say too much.

'I'm no good at Latin.'

He laughed. 'So what?'

'I've been to some parties and dances, quite fun, but I haven't done much work.' How could she get onto a more interesting, adult conversation? She twisted her thick hair up and then let it flop down around her shoulders, a habit she wished she could stop doing.

'Parties?' he said, wiping a tomato stain from his blue shirt. 'Lucky you.'

She felt briefly sympathetic, and then puzzled. Did parties matter once you were his age and married? What was she doing studying *Beowulf* and Chaucer for the next three years? She looked around the small restaurant. She'd always hated flock wallpaper.

'How are things at school?' she asked. Why had she agreed to meet him? An image of Theresa's face swam into her head. Theresa had sent her a postcard from Oxford saying she was having a brilliant time, which Shirley couldn't believe. Theresa should be here with Mr Williams, discussing Classics.

'School is fine,' he said. 'Unlike home.'

She wondered whether he'd told his wife about having lunch with an ex-pupil? Why wouldn't he tell her? They weren't doing anything wrong.

'Angela is rather down in spirits,' he said. 'Depressed, I suppose.' He removed his glasses, folded them, put them on his side plate, then undid and pulled off his tie. Shirley looked carefully at him for the first time. She'd always glanced sideways when she'd been in the classroom with him, missing his gaze, keeping him at a distance. He had a nice-shaped face, brown eyes, and a medium-sized nose. She noticed a twitch above his left eyebrow.

She said, 'I'm sorry. But surely people don't get depressed for no reason.' She resolved not to get depressed herself, even over the shocking irrelevance of all she was now required to read.

'Her mother was also depressed. Was there a reason? I don't know. It's a family trait. Angela's mother killed herself in the end.'

Shirley was now very keen to leave and return to her hall of residence. She actually wanted to stand up and scream.

He asked her if she'd like coffee and she said she never drank it.

'I didn't ask you out to weigh you down with this,' he said. 'It's very nice to talk to someone who isn't involved.' He asked for the bill and insisted on paying, which Shirley let him do, thinking that her contribution was to be a diversion for him.

'I like your green dress,' he said, as she lifted her mac off the chair back and pulled it on, the loose dress sleeves catching in the tighter mac sleeves, so he had to help her. 'Party girl. Take me with you next time.'

Was he serious? 'Don't you need to rush off to your convention or whatever it is?' she said as they hovered uncertainly on the pavement outside the restaurant. He said he hoped she had time for the British Museum. She couldn't think of an excuse not to, and so agreed.

They walked around some of the galleries and spoke cautiously about the exhibits. Shirley wondered why it was OK to gawp at dried bodies, bones, skulls, simply because they'd been dead a very long time, hundreds or thousands of years, and because they came from far away, across the world. She started to say this to him, then stopped, because, for all she knew, it could be a much-debated subject she ought to know about.

Outside on the museum steps, he caught hold of her belt which was looped and buckled at the back of her mac and twizzled her round by it. She laughed as she wobbled precariously on the steps, and prepared herself to be kissed.

'Enough silliness!' he said letting her go, and not kissing

her. 'Let's walk in the little park and then I'll head for my train.' They walked to Russell Square gardens.

Shirley remembered that he'd had a car crash. Had he been injured? Had it affected his head?

They were standing in the shadow of a row of plane trees and she noticed their mottled trunks like army camouflage. A woman walked past being pulled along by a red-coated Corgi on a lead.

'She wants to have a baby but that hasn't happened,' he said.

Shirley said something sympathetic in response, but she couldn't appreciate the problem. Not everyone could have a baby, that was obvious, and probably a good thing. So why not just get on with life and accept your fate?

'She promised to come to London to see a doctor, for a second opinion,' he said. 'But then she refused, so I saw him on my own, before meeting you. Things are difficult between us.'

She didn't want to hear any more about their problems, so said nothing, just murmured her goodbyes. He took her hand, squeezed it, and walked away. Shirley hadn't had time to form expectations – the lunch date had been arranged in such a hurry – so she couldn't say she was disappointed.

Going back on the tube, she just sighed in relief that she'd got through it. She would take off the green velvet dress as soon as she got back, put on her old trousers and sloppy mohair sweater and slob around. It might be Saturday night but she was done with men. She'd have a can of something for a meal, if she could scrounge it from Mags. She yawned, realised she'd reached the Baker Street stop, and got off the tube. She'd start the essay tomorrow.

'That green dress really suits you,' Maggie said as Shirley walked into their room. 'It lights up your eyes.'

Shirley never knew how to take compliments. They hadn't exactly been bandied about at home, with two teasing brothers and parents who thought praise for her appearance would encourage vanity. 'It was my mother's, from yonks ago. She grew out of it.'

Then she noticed her roommate's eyes were ringed with shadows or smudged mascara, as if she'd been crying. 'Are you OK, Mags?' She'd always wanted a sister, and now here was someone very like a sister and she hardly had time for her. She made cheese on toast for them both and listened to Maggie's story about Tony, the boyfriend in the sheepskin coat, who wanted more freedom in their relationship which he said Maggie would find pleasurable if she just gave it a chance.

Shirley didn't complete her assignments until the last week of term, rushing through them at breakneck speed. At school, she'd often done her best work on a knife-edge, and she assumed she could carry on in this way. When she returned after Christmas she'd commit to the course and work hard.

The woman at the family planning clinic asked for too much information. Date of birth, marital status, home address.

'I'm nineteen,' Shirley protested. 'Surely, it's my decision.'

'You're under twenty-one,' the woman said. 'You're not married. That does make a difference.'

Shirley made an appointment with the college doctor instead. She expected a middle-aged man but the doctor was a woman. This was surprising, and nice. Dr Gray, wearing a grey velvet jacket with fur collar, appeared unshockable. She told Shirley about something called a cap. 'Better safe than sorry,' she said. 'There is something else you could try but it's still new and has side effects. This is more natural.' She smiled sympathetically. 'Make sure you read the instructions. A clever girl like you shouldn't have any problems.' Her straightforward approach was reassuring. 'It's usually best to have it in place in advance, rather than struggling with it during...'

Shirley struggled with it every morning that week, trying to fit it correctly and to ignore the sickening smell of the gel she had to smear on the flesh-coloured rubber pouch that would protect her cervix. Then it was the end of term and Ollie was busy writing essays for deadlines, and she was never given the chance to rely on the cap's protection. They agreed to return early to university, before the start of term, so they could have time together. Shirley decided to be patient.

The holiday passed quickly enough thanks to her job delivering Christmas post. Trekking along outlying lanes and up the steep hill on the west of town, laden with cards and parcels, dealing with locked gates, dogs and the darkness which came before she'd completed the afternoon delivery, gave her time to think. She enjoyed doing practical work in the here and now. Why was she wasting her life translating Old English? She couldn't imagine a more irrelevant subject. Why hadn't she considered the syllabus more carefully? She'd been too caught up in the excitement of leaving home. She tried to talk to her mother but she would have loved the opportunity to go to university and thought Shirley had her future all nicely mapped out.

'Once I've done my degree, I definitely won't carry on with Latin and Greek,' Theresa said as they sat with other school friends in the pub. 'I'm aiming for a post in the government.'

'Government?' Shirley couldn't think how to begin on that one.

'Civil Service,' Theresa replied.

'What about teaching?' Shirley asked.

'I have thought about it. Mr Williams doesn't seem that happy with his lot, does he?' Theresa said, relaxing into a favourite topic.

'It could be about something else, not school,' Shirley replied, feeling guilty about her extra knowledge. She wanted to tell her friend about the lunch, the museum, the walk in the park with Chris. But she couldn't bear to see Theresa's disappointment that Shirley was the one singled out by Chris. Instead, she said, 'I've got problems with my boyfriend.'

'I'm avoiding all that for now,' said Theresa. 'I'd hate to be stuck in a dead-end relationship. What's the point?'

What was the point? Good question. Ollie was lukewarm. She was uncertain about her course. How far had she gone along these two paths? Could she change tack?

Existential angst, she decided, having recently overheard someone discussing this idea.

'You've always been academic,' her mother had said. 'Always reading. We couldn't stop you. But if you don't like it, I suppose you can leave. Get a job. Don't know what they'll say about your grant money, mind.' Shirley blew her mother a kiss and disappeared upstairs to pack.

She wanted to study a modern subject, something like Sociology, which she'd hardly known about when she'd applied.

She wrote to Ollie explaining her worries. In return, she received a boring box of chocolates and a glitter-decorated card. He was sorry not to have been in touch, sorry her present was late, sorry to be such a let-down. His Christmas had been quiet. Good, Shirley thought. What he deserves. Make him appreciate me. The tedious cousins had visited. He hadn't found a holiday job and was broke. He wanted to see her. Unfortunately, he couldn't return to London early because his mother was very groggy with flu.

'The professor wants to see you.' Miss Bloom, department secretary, smiled knowingly at Shirley who had called in at the office to hand in her assignment, only a little overdue, and to collect the one on Milton's poetry she'd put in before Christmas. Shirley was bemused – had word got around that she wanted to change her course?

'Your work is well below the standard we expect,' the tall, austere professor said. She glanced disapprovingly at Shirley's long tangled hair. The professor's hair was short and white, not a strand out of place. She'd told the students that she considered long hair anti-feminist and a waste of time and energy.

Shirley started apologising, then blurted out she wasn't sure the course was right for her.

'It's a bit late to decide that,' the professor said. 'You've deprived another young person of the chance to study with us.' She sighed and picked up her fountain pen. Shirley said she would do better. 'It will need to be very much better. C minus is bad.' Shirley muttered agreement, shocked by her essay grade.

Feeling ashamed at her sudden descent into idiocy, she went straight to the students' union bar. She wouldn't let anyone know about her failure. No use crying. In the loo, she combed and smoothed her hair, applied lipstick and smiled into the mirror. Lucky she had the sort of face that didn't show her feelings. She'd have a drink and wait for Ollie to arrive.

She ignored Ollie's tense expression and hugged him warmly. 'How was Christmas? Tell me about it.' Sending her Cadbury's Milk Tray chocolates showed he'd been feeling very down.

'I got engaged to my home girlfriend, Elaine. I'm sorry,' Ollie said. 'I had to, we were sleeping together and her parents found out...they were very angry.' He looked embarrassed, but not as upset as Shirley thought he should. 'I had to tell you, don't want to deceive you anymore.'

'Married?' she couldn't take it in. 'Married? You're far too young.'

'Not yet, not for ages.' He smiled, now cheerful at having confessed. 'Don't think about it. I've been a let-down I know, I was worried, but it's sorted, I feel better. I want us to start again – please – I'm crazy about you, Shirley. Come to my room now, no-one's about.'

'You've got to be joking!'

Next morning, she bought a bunch of newspapers and searched through the job adverts. She'd start her studying again in the autumn, at a different university, different subject, more relevant.

Maggie was sitting at their shared desk and hardly raised her head from her work to say hello. A collection of stones and rock crystals were arranged in front of her.

'Coffee, Mags?' Shirley asked, placing a mug before her roommate who turned to her with a tear-stained face. 'What's wrong?'

'I've mucked everything up. I'm pregnant.'

'Is it Tony's?' Shirley asked then wished she hadn't because, of course, it must be.

Mags nodded. 'I think so.'

Shirley put her arms around her friend and hugged her tight. 'What are you going to do?'

'Abortion. If I can get the quack to do it.' Mags searched through her bag and produced a scrap of paper. 'Someone else used him. Not sure he's actually a doctor but how hard can it be?'

'Are you sure?'

'Wouldn't you do the same? I can't rely on…him… He'll run a mile.'

A few days later, Maggie returned from her early morning medical appointment whey-faced and hunched over. She perched gingerly on the edge of her bed.

Shirley had already packed her trunk and bumped it down the wooden stairs. She hoped the warden wouldn't notice it in the hall, by the phone cubicle, as she didn't want a difficult conversation with her.

'I'll make you some tea. Take aspirins,' she said, searching for some in her duffel bag.

'He said no pills, just rest, twenty-four hours, then I should feel better.' Mags groaned and lay back on the bed, pulling the quilt over her.

'Hot water bottle.' Shirley hurried into the tiny kitchen to boil a kettle. When she returned, Mags was retching into a towel. She was shaking and said she was freezing.

'You need a doctor. I'll get someone.'

'Don't. Please don't!' Mags grabbed Shirley's hand. 'I'll be OK in a few hours. It's like a very bad period, that's all.'

The university would chuck Mags out if they learned about the abortion.

'I'll come to see you later,' Shirley promised.

Shirley could simply abandon the university and not let them know until she was two hundred miles away. She was sick of their disapproval. But she decided to face it.

'You can't just leave, what are you going to do?' Miss Bloom, the secretary, said. 'It's too late to replace you. We won't have our full complement of students. Goodness me. The professor is away today but she would not like this.' She pulled a bulging orange cardboard file off a shelf, tipped out various forms, ran her finger down a list. 'I wonder…' she picked up the phone, glanced at Shirley, and waved her goodbye.

When she returned to their room, Maggie was asleep. Shirley tiptoed around collecting the rest of her things. She scribbled a note urging her to see a doctor and never mind what people say. 'Please look after yourself,' she wrote. 'The important thing is to STAY ALIVE.' Mags was the only person she would regret leaving and that was so typical of her life, a friendship developing too late.

She pushed a letter to the absent warden under the door to her flat.

In the taxi with her trunk, Shirley thought about the job – teacher of French and English at a private school in Cornwall, start as soon as possible. She'd embellished her work experience but on the phone the headmaster had sounded desperate for help and not too concerned that she lacked a teaching qualification – her A-levels would be fine, and at nineteen, she was old enough. He was enthusiastic about her Latin abilities. The job came with a flat.

Chris Williams had agreed to give her a reference, though very surprised by her decision. Although he couldn't quite see her as a teacher, he said he was sure she could manage. He said he would love to visit her once she'd settled in. This suggestion worried Shirley and she hadn't replied.

She hadn't yet told her parents about her decision, but

at least teaching was something they approved of. As she gazed out of the taxi window at the iconic buildings, she felt a lump in her throat now she was leaving the city she'd always wanted to live in. Would she ever be able to come back? Then her heart started thumping, thinking about Mags, lying in bed, not asking for help, getting worse, not better.

How could she abandon her? What was she thinking? The neglectful warden wouldn't check on her for days. There'd been girls at the university who'd died after abortions. Someone she'd talked to at the students' bar had subsequently bled to death in the bath. No one had discovered her till too late. She couldn't risk leaving Mags to that fate.

By the time she reached her destination, and found a phone, it would be much, much too late. Mags' survival was way more important than Shirley's temporary, unsuitable job, boring university course, or disloyal boyfriend.

The taxi was stuck in a traffic jam and the driver didn't seem surprised when she asked him to turn around and take her back to the place she'd come from. He dumped her trunk by the open front door. Shirley ran up the wide staircase and into the room where Mags was lying under a quilt and some blankets in bed, very still and cold to Shirley's touch. 'Why d'you come back?' she mumbled.

'Forgot my green dress,' Shirley said, opening the wardrobe door to check. She'd left it for Mags but now she realised it was a sort of talisman that she wanted to keep. Anyway, it had been her mother's. 'Really, I came back to sort you out, you dozy dope. You're very ill.'

After phoning 999 for an ambulance, Shirley went to the warden's room and managed to extract her departure letter from under the door, with the aid of a thin ruler. As usual, the warden was nowhere to be found when needed.

Shirley pushed to the back of her mind all thoughts about the future, the unravelling she'd have to do to stay at university after all, and transfer to another course. And what she would say to the head of the school in Cornwall who had been happy to take her on unseen as a fully-fledged teacher. Whatever happened, she was certain she wouldn't regret changing her plans in order to look after her friend. She waited impatiently by the front door for the ambulance, willing Mags to stay alive.

Great Barrier Reef

She tells her mother she's going to work – cook and general dogsbody – on a small cruiser going from Townsville up the east coast to Cairns. She wants to see something of Australia, wants to swim on the Great Barrier Reef, and working will help pay for the trip. When the boat work is done, she'll spend a few days in Cairns, take a train out to the rain forest, then return to Brisbane and a flight back to the UK.

'Why go all that way for a holiday?' her mother asks.

'I was almost born in Australia,' she replies, clattering the dishes as she takes them to the sink.

'If you're going looking for him, it'll be difficult. It's a massive continent, Elizabeth,' her mother says, not rising to help her.

'I'm not going looking for him.' She runs a sink of water and scrubs the plates and pans, there being no dishwasher in her mother's flat. She will only be gone three weeks, surely not too long, and she'll be back in time for her mother's next course of treatment.

It's daylight when the plane circles over Brisbane. The middle-aged man next to her has slept most of the journey, which is a blessing. After hours flying above reds and ochres, she's now gazing down at the sea, the estuary, boats, harbour cranes and buildings, the city skyscrapers. She has just one evening before returning to the airport and taking the plane to Townsville.

In the hotel room, it isn't worth unpacking. She changes into clean t-shirt and jeans and sets off.

She takes a taxi to the bar where they've arranged to meet. She'd never find it on foot, her head swimming with jet lag. She sits at an outside table on the boardwalk next to the river. The waiter brings a glass of cold beer and pushes a dish of cashews and macadamias across the table to her. Around her, are young workers in suits, linen dresses, or pressed shorts and deck shoes. She thinks about all the extra hours she's worked to pay for this. The setting sun casts shadows across tables and people.

While she waits, Elizabeth takes out of her rucksack: a photo, a Christmas card with a picture of a kangaroo, and an oval jade brooch. It's past six, the time they arranged to meet. She decides she will search the bar and restaurant inside when she's finished her beer. She'll be looking for a man like this – she picks up the black and white passport photo – her father then aged about forty. He has thick, light-coloured hair and hooded eyes that remind her of her own. She's never met him before, only has this photo, her mother's descriptions and the email from him saying he'll be wearing a green shirt.

Elizabeth opens the kangaroo card that's almost identical to all the other cards her mother's Aussie friend, Myra, sends each Christmas. This latest one is a little different because along with the usual, 'Merry Christmas, Susie, hope all is well with you!' there is Myra's email address.

'Apart from sending our usual card, I'm not getting in touch. She's trouble,' her mother said when she and Elizabeth were together in December. 'Myra had thirty years to tell me something interesting and she never did.'

Elizabeth contacted Myra and eventually spoke to her on the phone.

'I met your mother at the dress shop, then we became friends,' Myra said. 'That place sold everything but rarely anything a woman would want to wear. I felt sorry for her working there. No air-conditioning.'

'I don't suppose there were many jobs available then,' Elizabeth said, remembering what her mother had told her.

'Too right. Hey, look me up if you ever venture down-under.'

She places the photo and card back in their envelope, then picks up the soft green brooch which her mother gave her years ago and which she's somehow not lost in all her relocations.

It's nearly six-thirty and no sign of him. She's wearing the pink top she said she would. This must be the right place. It had to be – the taxi brought her to the address she was given. She leaves her novel, *The Narrow Road to the Deep North*, on the table and some beer in the glass to reserve her place as the bar has now filled up. She pushes past people as if heading to the toilets. It could be useful anyway as she'd like to check her hair and redo her lipstick. She looks around for a man who is now about seventy and will have grey hair or none, she supposes. She makes eye contact with a few men, which becomes embarrassing.

She sends a text message to her father. 'Where are you? Been here since six. Will stay another half hour, then go.' She wonders how long is long enough when it comes to waiting for him.

Next day, her flight from Brisbane is early so there's no chance to rearrange their meeting.

She leaves Townsville airport, takes a taxi, finds the boat and after brief introductions to the skipper and the crew, she stows her bags away in her small cabin. The twenty-five passengers will arrive soon, not as many passengers as usual because the weather has been unseasonably stormy. Maurice is the cook and she is his assistant.

'How long are you working on the Coral?' Maurice asks as they unpack supplies and stow away the vegetables, frozen fish, cartons and packs of food. He heaves a box of wine onto the counter.

'One way only, six days. See how it goes,' she says. That evening, she fries the fish until its skin is charred and the flesh dry shreds. She uses the same knife and board for chopping onions and strawberries.

'No offence, but you're not much of a cook,' Maurice says.

'I'm not a cook. Back home, I'm a paramedic,' she says.

'Why come all this way to slave in a ship's kitchen?' he asks.

They put together hot breakfasts, salad lunches, prawns in dressings, grilled mullet or snapper and chips for supper. She's polite to the passengers but doesn't converse much. They're here to have fun and she's a worker. She keeps cooking and clearing up while engaging in angry, imaginary debates with her father. Everything she wants to accuse him of, everything she's bottled up since she was a kid. She's come all this way and he doesn't bloody turn up.

'You all right?' Maurice asks as they stand together on deck watching for sharks, ready to sound the alarm, while the passengers swim and dive. 'I wouldn't say you're an extrovert.' He's looking through binoculars.

She laughs. He's no extrovert, either. She's watched him making hard work of chatting up one of the male passengers. 'I came over here to meet my father and he didn't show up,' she says.

'Was there a reason?' Maurice asks.

'He went to a different bar,' she replies. 'Then when he realised where I was, I'd gone. That's what he says.' She reaches into her pocket, retrieves her mobile and listens again to the short message he left her. At least it's his voice.

'That's a pity,' Maurice says, sympathetically. 'I mean – was there a reason you came all this way to meet him at this time?'

She says something non-committal, thinking: Is it because I have questions for him? Is it because I want to explore my Aussie genes? Am I coming here because Mum can't, or won't?

She pulls on the all-in-one net covering that goes over her swimsuit and protects her against biting fish, then clambers down the ladder to the water. She's never learned to scuba, can't bear the idea of being weighed down. Her instincts are to stay on the surface where she can breathe unaided or to hold her breath to dive down, which she does now to view a giant conch shell. Multi-coloured, glinting fish are everywhere. Now she's learned what to look for, she sees that the coral is a mixture of living and dead.

After six nights on board, she's adapted to the situation and can hardly face disembarking in Cairns. She'd rather do the journey over again: cook, shark-watch, swim and snorkel, visit tiny reef islands and walk the sandy, shrubby paths. She could keep doing the journey, never get off the boat, never go back.

But she doesn't want to waste her room booking and plane ticket, so she disembarks. Some of the passengers and crew are going to a 'shindig' at a place near the harbour and she's invited. As she leaves the quay, someone gives her a piece of paper with the details.

She goes by bus to the Oasis Holiday Apartment she's rented for a few days, and once settled into what is a no-frills bedsit, she strips off her jeans that smell of seawater and cooking, and puts on a flimsy dress, heels and some eyeliner.

As she walks to the party venue, she sends a text message to her mother telling her she's arrived safely in Cairns. She asks her how she's feeling but doesn't phone because she's not ready for a long, intense conversation.

The party is on one side of a restaurant in a room bedecked with 'Happy Birthday' bunting. There are drinks and bits of cheese and meat scattered over platters. She's arrived late and can't see anyone else from the boat but she guesses they could be standing near the bar.

She downs a piña colada then stops a passing waiter and grabs a large cocktail with fruit in it. That feels good, very good. She knows she mustn't drink too much but she needs to let go a little. She's done hundreds of night shifts to pay for this trip.

Adele's 'Hello' booms out and couples are dancing to the music on a small wooden dance floor. She's ready to chill but feels so disorientated.

For most of her life, she's heard nothing from her father. She doesn't count the early letters or the first birthday card he apparently sent, because her mother destroyed the lot when she was a toddler. Now she has his mobile number and she'll use it. She doesn't believe his feeble excuse for not turning up.

She begins her message: 'Why did you chuck Mum out? She loved you. Why didn't you look out for her or me? Her parents were useless, then you let her down. Fucking no-good—'

'Found your way here, then?' a man with tangled blond hair says, interrupting her. Does she know him? 'You seemed knackered when I gave you the invite.'

After three drinks, her brain scrambles to change tack from texting her father to being polite to this stranger. She shoves her phone back into her bag. 'Whose birthday is it?' she asks, sure she must have been told.

'Johnno's fortieth,' he says gesturing to a group over on the other side of the room. 'We were at school together.' He's standing too close. 'I invited you as a thank you for all you did for us on the *Coral*.'

'You're welcome. I'm not normally a cook, but—'

'Enjoy the trip?' he asks.

'I suppose so,' she replies. 'The snorkelling was amazing. The colours of those fish!'

'Fancy a dance?' he says, guiding her by the elbow towards the dance floor. They move around self-consciously to another Adele number. When the track changes, they get into it more. She starts laughing at the way he wiggles his hands above his head and then thinks – be careful not to hurt his feelings, he may be sensitive. But he doesn't seem offended by her laughter. She hopes they won't put on a slower number as she isn't ready for closer contact. She remembers one of her friends back home saying she might have a fling or even a romance on her trip. He leads her back to the more subtly-lit side of the room.

She doesn't know his name, feels embarrassed because surely he told her on the boat? She thinks it's on the slip of paper she was given.

Now she's starting a fourth drink which he picked up off the counter as they passed.

'Mind if I smoke?' he says, offering her a roll-up.

'Thank you, I don't. You go ahead.'

'I'll need to step outside,' he says. 'Like to join me? Bring your drink.'

It would be rude to decline as he invited her to this party, so she goes with him. The cocktails are strong and her determination seems weaker than usual. She quietly tips the remainder of her drink into a flower pot.

She fiddles with her bag, unclasping it, and then groping around to find that note he gave her which she can't find. 'I'm sorry – I've forgotten your name—' the words sound all wrong and he doesn't reply. She feels into her bag again. It's crammed with too many items so things start to fall out. Where's her mobile? She's just been using it and now it's disappeared.

'The sunset over the sea is beautiful tonight,' he says. His arm guides her out of the restaurant despite her attempts to put some space between them.

'I think something's dropped out of my bag. I need to find —' She's not used to going anywhere without her phone but perhaps it is there and she simply needs to keep looking.

A voice clamours in her head: Don't go any further with this stranger. But he seems nice enough and she doesn't want to annoy him.

'Grab a look at the view before the sun disappears. Then we'll go back to the party,' he says.

He amuses her with his imitations of the captain's early-morning announcements and barked-out instruc- tions on the cruiser. They are leaning against the restaur- ant's back wall, looking across the sea.

She tries to visualise him on board. Her head's gone fuzzy. Was he the guy who preferred his own company, sitting in a corner with a beer and an iPad? She's unsure.

'I must go back!' She hears a snatch of Bob Dylan growling something. Now he's steering her away from the restaurant and the party and along the pavement towards the main road. She knows she must get away, find her phone, sit down at one of those tables. But he's gripping her around the shoulders. He's forcing her in the direction he wants.

She tries to drag her feet, tries to scream, but it all seems so difficult, hardly a sound coming out of her mouth. She should be shaking with fear, not weirdly passive, her legs heavy, her head lolling.

She realises he's going to shove her into his car, drive them to God knows where. She'll need to throw herself out of the moving vehicle but the doors will be locked. She'll stagger to a petrol station, if there is one in the outback, plead for help or – and this is more likely – they'll end up at an empty warehouse where he'll tie her up, rape her, kill her.

She sees headlights flicking past on the road ahead. She doesn't even know his name.

'Hey you! Lady! This your phone?' A man runs out of the restaurant shouting and waving something. She thinks it's Maurice from the boat. She can just hear and see him as it's not yet pitch dark.

'She's not well, mate, been drinking, I'm taking her home,' her abductor shouts, pushing her along more roughly and further from the party and the man whom she sees now is not Maurice but a waiter from the restaurant.

'No! No!' But it's just a whisper. 'Help please!' She makes her legs buckle.

'Fuck you,' her abductor says. 'Move.'

'Saw you at the party,' the waiter shouts. 'You dropped this. It's yours. Yours!' He runs towards them.

'I'll get her to the car then come back for it. Don't interfere.'

But the waiter won't be put off. 'You all right, you don't look too special?' he says as he reaches them, nimbly sidestepping as her abductor makes a grab at the phone he's holding.

The situation is obvious. Her abductor lets go of her, says he'll fetch the car, and disappears.

The waiter helps her back into the party. 'I think I've seen him try this on before,' he says. 'Screwed-up guy. Watches out for boat parties and crew like you. Probably spiked your drink. I'll phone the police.'

'Don't,' she says. 'It's my…fault. I'm. I'm all, all right. I need to be more careful.' It's difficult to talk, her words slurring and she's shaking but it's likely shock not cold.

'I'll bring you a coffee,' he says.

'You saved me,' she says. 'Thank you, thank you.' Tears trickle down her face as he makes her a coffee. She drinks it immediately, welcoming the scalding bitterness.

'We'll sort out that guy, don't you worry,' he says. 'We'll report him. He'll be on camera.'

If she hadn't been trying to text and then fumbled putting her mobile away, so that it fell from her bag, if the kind waiter had delayed a few more minutes, even a few seconds… She's very grateful to him.

She scrolls down to erase the message she planned to fire off to her father. To her horror, she sees it has been sent. She must have accidentally pressed send when she was interrupted.

'I shouldn't have sent that message,' she writes in a text.

'It's only what I deserve, Liz,' he types back, 'after everything.'

She agrees to meet him at the botanical gardens when she returns to Brisbane.

Her few days in Cairns are spent in her room, sleeping, or hiding in cafes. She doesn't go to the rainforest. She doesn't walk along the beach because there are warnings everywhere about crocs. She is on the lookout for the giant spiders she's heard about. She's relieved her room is high up in the block.

She dreads coming across that man again. She doesn't want to talk about the attack. The only person she could possibly confide in is Maurice and he's gone, the cruiser already making its way back south, weaving between the islands, putting down anchor for swimmers and divers to enjoy the reef.

She phones her mother to tell her when she'll be arriving home. Her mother asks, 'How is he?'

'If you mean Dad, I haven't met him yet,' she replies.

'There's no need to make contact with him on my account,' her mother says. 'I have you. I have my friends. I had my hard times and I've come through.' There's disappointment in her voice.

There is something Elizabeth believes she could do for her mother: phone Myra and get some answers. It will be easier to do when her mother isn't in the same room, but rather on the other side of the world.

'Why doncha take the train here?' Myra asks. Elizabeth murmurs a reply but she knows she won't go. It's so far, and she doesn't have time. She doesn't tell Myra about her mother's illness, because that's private and not for her to discuss. She takes a big breath and asks Myra about her father's other family.

'Family? I wouldn't call it 'family!" Myra says, cackling and then coughing her smoker's cough down the phone. 'There was a woman, way back, but that's history. She caused your dad some grief, that's for sure. I tried to tell your mother, but she couldn't bear to hear it. I probably didn't use the right words.'

'Any children?' Elizabeth asks, as casually as she can.

She's sitting on the grass near the circle of palm trees where they agreed to meet. The gardens are beautiful but crowded as it's the weekend. The sky is azure and the sun brilliant. It will burn her skin if she doesn't cover up.

She won't tell her father about her near-abduction at the party in case he forms the wrong opinion of her. She won't tell him her mother never found a serious partner in the three decades since she left Australia because that seems to reflect badly on her and she is an attractive, kind woman.

Elizabeth wonders what they can talk about, what would be worth saying. She unwraps a wedge of tomato and avocado sandwiches she made this morning and which she intended to share with him. She nibbles one, scatters the crumbs across the grass.

He didn't believe her mother was pregnant, not until her bump showed, then he made her go. She went back home to the other side of the world.

'I was hasty,' her mother confessed to her recently. 'I didn't want to force him. In a way, I understood. With his background, on the farm, the harshness of it. Floods, fires, droughts. A family wasn't what he wanted.'

She imagines asking him, 'Am I your only child?' She knows the answer – Myra has told her – but she wants to hear him say that she is his only child. Not that she's a child, she's nearly thirty.

Some little birds with yellow wings fly down from a blossoming tree to inspect the sandwich crumbs. She thinks about forgiveness, what it would taste like.

She hears kids in the distance splashing through the fountain water.

She imagines him saying, 'Liz, thank you for finding me,' and herself replying, 'That's fine. I'm Elizabeth, not Liz.' She will show him the jade brooch he gave her mother when she moved in with him. She may take some photos of him.

She sees a man walking on his own around the palms. He's clean-shaven with white cropped hair, shabby beige chinos and a green checked shirt. He stops every now and then, raising his hand to shade his eyes, looking in one direction then another. She imagines he's looking for a tall, auburn-haired girl, someone like her mother. But Elizabeth is small like him. In a while, she may stand up and wave because she's almost certain he is her father. But for now, she sits perfectly still, pulling the peak of her cap down lower over her face to shield it.

Blue Lias

'You can't go back, Annie,' Caroline said. 'Well, of course, you can,' she qualified in her pedantic way, 'but—'

Her dark hair had frizzed up around her face and raindrops fell onto the table as she spoke.

'It wouldn't work,' I said.

She nodded vigorously and picked up the ammonite we'd just purchased at the museum. 'Don't look back. Don't get stuck in the past.'

She was trying to help me.

I understood perfectly why Caroline had been so lucky in love. Although not exactly pretty, she had a friendly appearance, was honest and loyal, and she knew her own mind. What more could any man want? I envied her life even though mine probably seemed fine to outsiders.

The kids I taught probably thought I was already a fossil, a dinosaur, at thirty-one years old.

We gazed out at the rain lashing down the café windows. We'd had to abandon our walk along the seafront. I wanted to treat her to tea and cakes before we went back to her tiny cottage crammed with babies and a husband who worked from home with varying success. The reunion was a great way for me to spend time with them, as well as to reconnect with other friends I'd lost touch with.

'Coming here, driving down the narrow main street, seeing the Cobb…it hit me worse than I thought it would.' Over the years I'd been careful never to return, even though I only lived in Somerset.

She murmured something sympathetic. 'You don't have to go. You could get back into your car and drive home. It's only a college reunion, not an invitation to Buckingham Palace.'

'If you hadn't told me he'd be there,' I moaned, thinking how I'm fatter, older, a primary school teacher, and have nothing of any interest whatsoever to talk about, whereas he….

'You look great,' she said firmly. 'Your new haircut really emphasises your cheekbones and your lovely green eyes.'

The reason she'd been lucky in love was because she knew herself, knew who would suit her, and she had gone for him. She had not been deflected.

'You can't have been really right for each other,' she said, 'or you would have found a way. Don't worry. There's somebody out there for you. Maybe tonight…'

It was June. We'd finished our exams and come on an end-of-year outing to a shingle beach at Lyme Regis. There were seven of us including Caroline and Danny – my gorgeous new boyfriend.

We'd met when we'd been on opposite sides of a debate about love, that hackneyed proposition that it was better to have loved and lost than never to have…well, you know it, and you can imagine the points that were made by a roomful of nineteen and twenty-year-olds.

I was too shy in those days to say more than a couple of sentences and I only made myself do it because I wanted to be a teacher and I reckoned I had to get used to public speaking.

Dan and I walked around the sloping beach, collecting driftwood and dried seaweed, piling it up into a great bonfire. Caro and the others unwrapped sausages, chopped salad, buttered bread, opened bottles and propped them upright with large stones. Then they wandered about looking for fossils, tapping with a hammer that someone had brought, their calls and laughter reflecting the relief that exams were over and the holidays beginning.

'What sort of grades do you think you'll get?' I asked Dan as we lit the fire and stood with our arms around each other.

'I don't care about my results,' he said which surprised me because I thought he was ambitious. 'But I do care about you, Annie.'

Our relationship had galloped along after that first meeting – as can happen when two young people spend a large part of every day and night together, even revising at the same table in the library. We'd hardly argued about anything since that first debate.

I envisaged our final year much the same and then moving in together as we started our first jobs, our first year of real independence. We loved each other; we were twin stars, two halves of an apple.

'I've got something to ask you,' he said, heaving another boulder to form an edge to the fire, 'something important.' He raked both hands through his vivid red hair. I held my breath. The sea made a distant lapping swish, and seagulls cried their messages.

'I'm leaving uni. I've decided to go to Oz. Hitch up with Dad.'

'Your Dad? Australia? You haven't seen him for years.' I heard sobs rise up in my throat.

'I know, but I want to make my way in the world, not study books, geography. I can do real geography, look after the land and earn at the same time. He's got me a job on his farm.'

'You have a great opportunity to get a degree, better yourself, but you can't hack it, can you, Daniel?' That sounded so like my snobby parents. 'Sorry. It's just...' I swallowed hard, 'so unexpected.'

'Annie, I want you to come with me,' he continued, his voice intense. 'We could get married, we're old enough. I want us to emigrate. Together. I want to make a life for us. Please.'

'Married? I'm not ready for that. And what about my music degree?'

He knew I found home life difficult. He probably thought I'd jump at the opportunity. Once I'd got over the shock, I did. I agreed to go with him.

'What happened then, in a nutshell?' Caro asked as we walked back along the promenade. 'Why did you guys split up?'

She'd played her part in all that. Didn't she remember the lecture she'd given me about valuing myself, not chasing after a man?

I noticed the Victorian-style street lamps, black against the pink sky, their shaded lights hanging from curled metal ammonites. The evening air was chilly, damp. The weak sun glinted over the sea and on the rocks, the Blue Lias of the distant cliff, picking out the layers and layers of time.

It was all right for her. She hadn't been faced with the conflict of having to choose between family and boyfriend.

'In a nutshell…' I said, and had an immediate image of Danny pulling down a branch, showing me the cluster of hazelnuts with glossy shells, perfect and strong. I remembered our argument and the way we'd parted. 'My parents were dead against the idea. Said we were too young. Wanted me to continue with my degree – that was important to them. Plus, they didn't really like him, thought he came from the wrong sort of family, and Dad has always had a thing against people with red hair. In the end, I gave in.'

We turned the corner to Fisherman's Cottage. 'I must just warn you,' she said, 'Hugo is pretty depressed about losing his job. But we're OK.'

'I'd like to do a boat-building apprenticeship,' her husband explained, 'but with all the unemployment round here, who's going to take me on?' We'd put the children to bed and now Caro was reading them a story.

He handed me a glass of the red wine I'd brought. 'Great to see you. Here's to life, love and…work.'

I thought about Dan, how concerned he'd been about finding work and earning a living, and how lacking in understanding I had been.

'Are you still playing the piano?' Hugo asked.

I told him how my music hadn't flourished, how I'd got my teaching qualification belatedly, and how I liked the children but not the admin, the usual sort of teachers' complaint.

'And what about your man?'

'What man?'

'I can't remember his name – isn't he in an orchestra? Why didn't you bring him along?'

I muttered something about that relationship being over.

'Time to go,' Caro said, ushering the babysitter into the living room and whispering, 'They're asleep – but here's our mobile number.'

'I can't understand why Danny has come from the other side of the world for this reunion,' Hugo continued as the three of us climbed the steps to The Bay View Hotel where the party was taking place. 'Unless it's because he wants to see you, Annie.'

'Didn't I tell you?' Caro replied. 'His email said he was coming over here anyway, for a wedding. For all we know, it could be his own.'

'Why didn't you tell me this when we were in the café?' I snapped, angry, not just with her, but also with myself. I had no right to expect him to be single.

'Because you'd have gone home, Annie, and I didn't want you to.' She squeezed my hand. 'Don't think too badly of me.'

It was a decade since he'd left. Australia had seemed such a distant place to me then, somewhere I knew little about. I'd learned more in the intervening years from Aussies who were over here teaching or working in bars. But I'd never been there myself. Images of drought, floods and wildfires were graphic reminders of the extremes of nature. A farmer out there would need to focus on the essentials in life, I thought, not fuss on about what might have been.

Not a word had been exchanged between us since that last weekend when I'd told him that I was going to do what my parents wanted and continue at Exeter, get my degree. That I wasn't going with him after all. He hadn't contacted me once he arrived, not an email, not even a Christmas card. I got a few snippets of information from friends but, eventually, these dried up. He blanked me as if I'd never existed. I had thought we felt the same about each other, but I'd been wrong. I was too hurt to get in touch with him.

'It was never really serious with that musician, Hugo,' I explained as we stood looking out through the picture window at the expanse of sea, the dark walls of the Cobb, a few lights here and there, fishing boats setting out. What was I saying? This was a man I'd briefly been tempted to marry. 'He came from a wealthy background, and my father liked him. But I knew that wasn't enough.'

I couldn't settle for second best after what I'd had with Dan…Dan whom I could now see over the other side of the room, talking to people he seemed to know. He wasn't as tanned as I expected. Slim, tall. My heart lurched and pounded. Don't, I warned myself. You're an adult now. Calm down.

'Caro and I were sorry to hear about your mother,' Hugo said.

'Yes, it was horrible. I guess I needed a shoulder to cry on, and he was around. That's probably why the relationship went on, but it's all over now.' If Dan had stayed, if he hadn't abandoned me….

I stopped and took a deep breath. The last thing I wanted was to burst into tears at this reunion. I really did need to put the past behind me. 'I'm sorry, that sounded awful. I'm so angry with myself. Why didn't I trust my own judgement? It's not as if I've achieved anything in the last decade. With hindsight, I should have made a different decision and gone with Dan to Australia.'

'You put your life on hold for years, to care for your mum,' Hugo said, hugging me. 'What could be a better use of time than that? And by all accounts, she wasn't the easiest person to nurse.'

It was a relief to unburden myself to Hugo, and easier to talk with the music and hubbub around us. Perhaps it was easier with him than with Caro because he had suffered his own reversals. 'There's never been anyone else for me since Danny,' I said. 'No one. But he won't understand that. He's a man. Men are pragmatic.' I nearly said: men are arrogant.

'Whoa!' Hugo held his hand up. 'You can't speak for all men like that.'

I'd been so caught up in my own emotions that I hadn't seen Dan coming towards us. His eyes were burning into me. I couldn't look at him. Hugo slipped away through a group of people.

'I heard what you just said.' His voice had that familiar intensity and also, now, an Australian twang. 'It shocked me.'

I couldn't reply. Would it be a mistake to say I regretted my early, youthful decision? Don't look back. Don't get stuck in the past. Move on.

'I couldn't stay angry for all that time,' he said. 'But when I stopped, you'd found someone else.'

'You made your decision to go!' I hit back. 'Didn't discuss it with me first. Why didn't you wait? What about my plans?'

He stared into his pint as if trying to spot something very precious at the bottom of the glass. 'I guess I was young. And broke. And very foolish. I'm sorry for it. I've been pretty lonely as a result, you may be glad to know.'

I felt a rush of forgiveness that was completely unexpected, also a sense of shame as I recalled my own harsh words to him before he went. And then I wanted to laugh out loud. It was so wonderful to see him again.

'I'm sorry, Dan. But I was young, too, and thought I was doing the sensible thing. Even though—' But I didn't want to get into the whole thing about my parents' unhappy marriage. 'Aren't you getting married yourself, soon?'

'What? Me? No! My sister is.' He looked embarrassed, but continued firmly. 'What you decided wasn't wrong. If you'd come with me then, you wouldn't have been here for your mum. D'you know, you were always a very kind person, Anne. That was a quality I loved in you.'

Loved. 'I heard you've done well and have your own farm.' I hoped that sounded generous, not envious. 'We mustn't look back or get stuck in the past,' I said, to protect my feelings.

'We're not getting stuck. Or shall I say, I'm not. We're different now,' he said.

My first love would always be completely special to me. We were who we were today, because of the past.

I wouldn't change our history, even if I could. Like the layers of Blue Lias in the cliff, one era was always built on the previous one.

Now, we must trust that something good will come from what we've been through. We try not to beat ourselves up about the past and hope we'll be able to work out a way of being together.

Northern Lights

There was a polar bear in reception. Its beady eyes, sharp-toothed grimace, and outstretched paws sent shivers down her spine. It was only a stuffed bear, but life-sized, enormous. Maybe it was the minus ten degrees that made her shiver. Icicles hanging in points off roofs, glassed-over pavements, the dark sky at three p.m. Or maybe it was the prospect of spending a week in close quarters with a man she was in the process of separating from. As they waited silently together to get their room key, the wind whipped through the revolving door and into the lobby, making the fierce line of flames in the heater shudder.

'Why on earth are you going on holiday with him?' her father asked her in the week before she set off.

'You know why,' she said. 'The holiday was a present from Mum. She always wanted to see the Northern Lights.' Nina remembered her mother saying, just before she died: You go for me. It will be magical. Fjords, snow, swirling green skies.

'But you and Alex are splitting up,' Dad said, looking puzzled.

'Yes,' Nina snapped. 'The spark's completely gone.' Nina was trying to control her temper. 'But Mum loved him and he loved her so I'm doing it for them.'

She didn't say, because she couldn't, that she felt guilty about what had happened between her and Alex. She'd been unfaithful to him and had kept it secret. This holiday was her way of making some sort of recompense.

Mum had thought Nina and Alex were perfect together and it was obvious she was hoping they'd get married and have children, the unlikely fairy-tale ending.

Nina blinked away tears and said, 'Don't worry, Dad, it'll be OK but I can't carry on living with someone who works all the time, even on Christmas Day!' Alex was an ambulance controller. When she saw a shadow pass over her father's face she said, 'Of course, I didn't mean that. He does a brilliant job.'

A week was only a tiny fraction of her life. She was sure she and Alex could manage to be polite to each other for that length of time. When all this was over and she'd moved her books, clothes and Mum's china out of their apartment, she'd begin the rest of her life.

The hotel room where they'd booked for the first night was adequate. When she peered out of the dusty window to the street below, she read the sign on a shop window, 'Arctic Tattoo.'

Tattoo. The drums beating the end of their relationship. Tattoo, the pricking of skin, the indelible patterns that scarred you for life. Perhaps Alex would like to have a heart with their initials entwined. Yeah, right.

Was it possible to rekindle their relationship? She didn't

know. She remembered Mum so ill in hospital at the end, and she, Nina, going off with an ex she should have known was no good. She'd been completely out of her mind with grief.

'Don't just stand there,' Alex said, hanging up his jacket and fleece. 'Do something useful.' He stared at her. She drew the brown curtains across the window. His intense gaze had delighted her once. Now she felt he was putting her under a microscope, and finding her wanting.

The next day, Alex refused to visit the Polar Museum, so she went alone and watched a film about the brilliant night-time aurora. If they didn't get to see the real thing she'd at least have these images. It fitted. She'd stopped experiencing things for real and was being fed them second-hand. The sooner she could jump into her own skin the better. Just six more days, then she could leave him.

Things with Alex had been lacklustre for about six months then, when her mother became ill, Nina found herself getting angrier and angrier, which he didn't seem to understand or be able to cope with. Then she'd bumped into Stuart, and had fallen again for his casual charm.

Her Norwegian being non-existent, she read the English explanations by the displays. In what ways are polar bears, glaucous gulls and humans similar? She had no idea. Glaucous. It sounded yucky like mould or spit. Gull. To fool, deceive, or be deceived. She remembered this from studying Shakespeare way back.

She couldn't stand the way her circling mind always returned to the same thing. She wanted to scream at her thoughts, I can't do anything about it! It happened! Yes, I deceived him.

The answer to the question on the display was that polar bears, glaucous gulls and humans are all at the top of food chains and so are the creatures most affected by pollution. Bears and gulls innocent; humans guilty.

'I am guilty,' Nina whispered to herself as she wandered around the displays in the museum. 'Polluting and destroying the earth that feeds me.' These thoughts piled on top of her feelings about Alex, and what had happened when her mother was in hospital.

That evening, they made their way to the ship moored at the quay, up the gangway and into the warmth and hubbub. They found their cabin.

How did she get herself into this situation, with a man who didn't like her, and in a place where it was dark for twenty hours a day?

'Are we sitting together for dinner?' he asked without looking up from *Northern Lights*, the children's book he'd become obsessed with. If she opened her mouth to breathe she would scream, rip the wretched paperback out of his hands and chuck it the length of their very small cabin, so she said nothing.

The info about table seating showed they were placed with the same two people every night. In happier times Alex would have said, 'I just want to be on my own with you.' And she'd have been delighted. Now he just said, 'OK then.'

The older married couple they were seated with were both tax inspectors and had a fund of stories about celebrities and the dodgier side of accountancy.

'What's the difference between the Great Train Robbers and the Inland Revenue?' the husband asked as Nina chewed cured reindeer.

As she didn't know, she replied with her own question, 'How long can a polar bear go without food?' While the couple thought about this, and as Alex gazed away from them and at the young woman at the next table, she continued, 'Seven months. Amazing how humans can go without food for ages, too. What about that man who got stuck in his car covered in snow? How long was it? Two months?' Nobody quite knew. 'It's incredible how long we can actually go without what we think of as the essentials of life.' She looked pointedly in Alex's direction. How long had she gone without sex, kindness, love?

'The Inland Revenue didn't get caught,' the husband explained, laughing, then coughing, his face getting redder and redder. Nina didn't get the joke.

His wife asked, 'How long have you two been together?'

'Four years,' Nina said. Alex wasn't a totally bad person but she didn't love him, didn't even like him now. People get together for all sorts of reasons, not all of them right.

'I never wanted to come on this trip with you,' she said when they got back to their cabin. 'It's a mistake and I can't stand it any longer!'

'Get off the fucking boat then!' he shouted.

'We're at sea and it's freezing. I'm not swimming away.'

She remembered the day her mother went into hospital and the speed with which she'd deteriorated. The nurse saying gently, 'I'm going to move her into her own room.' Even then they didn't know what this meant. If she had known she would have been there all the time for Mum. She wouldn't have got side-tracked. She wouldn't have wasted time having one more drink, switching off her mobile.

'Let's try to get along,' she said when they got into their single berths and she felt calmer.

'You misled me,' Alex said. 'I thought you wanted me and you didn't. You were just marking time with me.'

'I certainly wasn't marking time with you,' she said, stung by the criticism. 'When we first moved in together, it was brilliant.'

'That was then,' he said. 'What about now? Why's it changed?'

She started to argue that relationships take two but she stopped herself. She'd made a mistake. They'd made mistakes. Then somehow they'd become trapped.

Next day, standing outside in the glacial air, with her back to the view of snow-packed mountains and groups of houses painted red, cobalt, mustard, she said, 'It's to do with grief.' He was looking through binoculars, the wind was howling and so he didn't hear. She continued. 'We need time.' She meant – to mourn.

But he said, 'Yeah. Marking time. Like I said.'

'Alex, please. I didn't mean that.' But he went to the other side of the boat to look at an oil rig.

She remembered she'd read that polar bears were becoming much more aggressive because everything was being taken away from them. She had turned into a raging polar bear.

The tax inspector lady came over to talk to her. 'Now that we're actually on board, our guide is describing them as the 'elusive' Northern Lights. I didn't see a thing last night, did you?'

'I think we've got the wrong sort of camera,' Nina replied. 'It can't capture the colours. Everything's grey.'

At midday, when they docked at a small town, she disembarked on her own, treading gingerly over ridged snow towards a white church on the hill. It was modern, built after the town had been razed to the ground during World War Two. All week they'd been learning about the horrendous things Norwegians had endured during that time.

Once inside, the rays of light streaming through the brilliant stained-glass windows – red apples in green leaves, a fish, dove, and holly wreath – all this made her gasp. Spring sunshine brightening and warming everything when she'd least expected it.

She lit a thin white candle and placed it with others in the metal ring, whispering a prayer for her parents. She didn't ask for anything for herself. Then she sat for a while in one of the painted wooden pews. She wasn't religious, but if she had been it would be this sort of calm, unpretentious church she'd choose. A little boy had followed her in and now observed her shyly. She sighed. Maybe she wouldn't have children now. He watched her as she dropped coins into the box. He tried to explain to her in his basic English about why they'd built the church.

He reminded her of her brother, Chris, as a kid. She'd go to see him soon, even though he didn't seem to need her. They were both good at disguising their feelings.

The nurse said she shouldn't blame herself, it often happened. Dad had been there but had just slipped out to get Mum some clean clothes. Alex had been on a 999 call, and Chris was on his way.

But she did blame herself because she'd been with that no-good man Mum detested. How and why had she done that? Wasting time in a nondescript pub, and elsewhere, while Mum was dying.

When Nina got back to the ship, Alex was downing a beer in the bar and watching wrestling on TV. She sat down at the small table. 'This is terrible. We're tearing each other apart.'

He mumbled in agreement. She continued: 'I'm not over Mum, and I know you're not. You got along so well. She was very fond of you.'

'It's not enough,' he said, and she knew he was right.

'Maybe for some people it would be enough, but not for us,' she replied.

'We can't stay together just because she wanted us to,' he said, apparently willing her to disagree.

She remembered something she'd read about there always being one person who loved more and one who loved less in any relationship. He deserved better.

'I wish I'd been there for her,' she said.

'You were on that work training day,' he said, and she kept quiet. 'I wish I hadn't gone on that call. Bloody Sir Galahad,' he continued. 'Not. I'm going to find a better job. So I don't have to work Christmas Day. Would that help us?'

'You mustn't do that – you do a great job! You saved a child's life. It was the only good thing that came out of that night.'

She wanted to tell him everything – about how she'd met Stuart in the street, and because she was sad and frightened about her mother, she'd opened her heart to him, and he'd used that vulnerability to do what he'd always done in the past, promising her the world. Then when he'd aroused her feelings for him, he disappeared over the horizon.

Confessing to Alex might make her feel better, but not for long. It would just start another cycle of anger and hurt. She had an image of a polar bear, maddened by hunger, pollution and melting ice-caps, ripping through snow, woods, streets, grabbing people, eating them, chucking the bones into icy fjords. She had an image of the boy in the church and his few stilted words: 'War – bad – then church – we do this church. Here.'

She supposed there was always a choice after war – forgive or at least try to understand, and then build something new. Let in the bright sun.

They didn't have to go on ripping into each other.

She picked up Alex's hand. 'I'm truly sorry it hasn't worked out. It's my fault.' This was so much easier to say than she'd feared. When the words came out, the tightness in her chest eased.

She was beginning to forgive herself. She could feel her heart slowing, her muscles relaxing, warmth spreading through her body. Spring sunshine on frozen winter earth.

'No, it's my fault,' he said, lacing their fingers together. 'I thought you were the one. Put too much on to you.' After a silence, he added: 'As long as we do get to see those 'elusive' Northern Lights, the trip will be worth it.'

'We'd better go out. Start looking at the sky,' she said, at last feeling that, perhaps, they would find their way through.

A Few Vital Minutes

Every morning Brendan did the counting game. He asked himself, if he had three minutes to live, what would he do? That thought, which was always the first into his mind, was enough to get him focused, sweating a little, muscles tensing, eyes open, and then he'd jump out of bed. His day had started.

He would find his mobile, switch it on, if it wasn't already, fill the kettle with filtered water, make a call. His parents, elderly, hard of hearing, and on the other side of the world, would be unlikely to get to their phone in time, especially in the middle of their night. So he'd call his ex-wife, leave a message if she didn't answer. He was on better terms with her these days.

Three minutes left of your life – that really concentrated the mind. But only if you knew.

He'd make a cup of tea, and drink it in the fresh air just as he was going to do now. There wouldn't be time to do more.

He went into the tiny kitchen, which was simply a curtained-off sink and a few cupboards in the corner, and plugged in the kettle. He was lucky to have electricity here. Lucky to have a mobile connection.

Then he thought, if he had just seven minutes to live, if by some weird chance the gods gave him notice, he would rush round to his next-door neighbour, and together they'd have a smoke, then that would be that.

Seven minutes was not enough to do anything much.

Although he'd never done well at exams, Brendan had always been very into maths. He admired its symmetry and logic. And so the next number he mused about, as he drank his sweet, scented chai was, as usual, twenty-one.

Twenty-one minutes was a very long, or a hideously short, period of time. It depended how you looked at it. Depended on how you used it, he thought, opening his tin of tobacco.

Twenty-one minutes wasn't quite enough time to hurtle up the coast on the largely unsurfaced road in his car which was currently under repair, collect his daughter from nursery school and drive her to a safer place. So he was working on this problem.

When he'd been at school, lessons had been endless in their boredom. He'd read somewhere that no one could concentrate on a subject for longer than twenty minutes at a time and he thought that was way over-optimistic. Twenty minutes, or even twenty-one, when he was a child, was often an eternity.

He admired the brilliant pink frangipani draped around his doorway. It had taken several years of coaxing to get the flowers to grow. While standing there, he noticed also a thin trail of smoke curling its way upwards in the distance, probably someone barbecuing chicken on the beach.

The pigeons were burbling in the trees, a parakeet screeching from roof to roof, and also he could hear the *click, click, clickety-click*, of frogs in bushes heavy with dew.

On that particular day, the day when the numbers game started, the birds had fallen suddenly silent, as if before a tropical downpour. He remembered noticing that, but he knew now that he only remembered because of what came after. He'd gone outside, sulkily, to watch Maya set off.

There was a long, eerie silence, and then a dramatic loud flapping, interspersed with hoarse caws, an amateur orchestra tuning up in the sky, as a dark cloud of birds, in clumps according to their species, thousands of them, winged their way to the hills. He'd stood and watched them, marvelling at what he thought was a seasonal occurrence. Maya had carried on walking up the hill.

He'd checked his watch – it was seven thirty-three a.m.

He hadn't even been a year on the island, had a very scanty knowledge of its history, geography, or people, so he didn't realise the strangeness of the birds' behaviour.

He'd gone travelling to escape from a stifled life and a failed marriage. After a month away, he'd been mugged on the mainland, and so with his last few notes and coins, he'd taken a cheap boat trip to these islands, which he'd never heard of before, found a bit of a job cleaning up after tourists, met a girl, started buying beads, and stayed.

That was one way of looking at it – everything happening by chance, a string of events thrown together. But sometimes he thought it all had more significance. That some being had strung the events together in a meaningful pattern.

On that particular day, five years previously, Brendan had been sorting through the beads he'd bought at the market in the city, dividing them up into sizes, colours, rarity, value, and so on, separating jade, garnet and lapis lazuli. He was looking through the small list of jewellers he was starting to supply back home, deciding on allocations and prices.

Life had begun to open up for him in a way he'd never dared hope for. But afterwards, when everything was lost, he'd had to go back to the beginning, and way before that.

He'd managed to get Maya interested in stringing together some necklaces, and even designing more ambitious items, with a view to her making an income. But they'd had a quarrel the evening before and so she'd got up early that morning, dressed the baby and whispered goodbye.

As the birds flew overhead, he'd watched her stepping quickly up the steep path out of the village to the road where the ramshackle bus stopped. In those days, he didn't have a car or any form of transport.

That morning, the tide was very far out, exposing a ridge of brownish, purplish rocky stuff he thought might be coral. There was a strong smell of seaweed.

She didn't like arguing, used to agree with most things he said or wanted but something had got to her. She'd said she needed time away. She'd decided to visit her family further along the coast, taking baby Lily with her.

Then, he'd been living in a different home from this one, one in a row of shacks almost on the beach, renting out to cash-strapped travellers. Now, these had all gone, and for a couple of years they hadn't been missed at all as there were no travellers, tourists or owners of huts.

Maya and Lily had only been gone three minutes and he knew that if he ran after them, he could catch them up. He was confident she wouldn't take much persuading to return with him. They'd go together to visit her family, another time.

Regrettably, he wasted a precious seven minutes more through putting the beads away, and hiding them under bedding, then packing a bag before trekking up to the bus stop. Their quarrel was his fault – he already felt very sorry. He felt abandoned.

She wanted to go to England with him, wanted a different life from the one her family had planned for her. She wanted to become a teacher. He agreed she was clever enough – she'd learned to speak and write English in no time. She wanted marriage.

It was unreasonable, he'd shouted at her the previous night. He'd been through all that before. They'd only known each other a short while.

Perhaps, she'd replied, winding her long brown hair into a twist and pinning it up to expose her slim neck and pointed little chin, but still they'd known each other long enough to have a baby, hadn't they?

It was a no-win situation for him. Her family didn't approve of him as a husband and they didn't approve of him not doing the right thing for their daughter.

In future, of course, he'd know the signs of a tsunami, he'd rehearsed them so well. Every day now he gazed, sniffed, listened. Every day, he walked several times along the shore, searching, collecting, staring at rocks, the line of the ocean, the bright sand strewn with wood, bits of huts, personal oddments like a plastic bowl, a salt-crusted boot.

That day, it took him longer than he'd expected to get to the bus stop because when he was halfway up the steep, stony path, he'd been knocked over by an enormous pack of barking dogs, pounding along as if they were being chased by a hunter, saliva dripping from their red jaws. They'd disappeared upwards, their barks echoing round the bay, becoming muffled and faint as they entered the forest in the centre of the island.

He'd picked himself up, shaken, but relieved the animals hadn't stopped to attack him, as rabies had always been one of his fears.

Of course, partly because of this upset, he missed the bus which had arrived and departed promptly at seven fifty-four a.m. What do a few minutes matter? Normally, nothing, on this island.

If he'd arrived at the stop just a couple of minutes earlier he could have boarded it and begged Maya to get off. That's what he would like to have the chance to do now.

Instead, he'd watched the bus disappearing along the road which meandered and dipped down closer to the coast.

Now, he would give anything to unreel those twenty-one minutes.

Then he'd heard the mighty growl. From his vantage point above the trees and vines, he saw a huge wall of boiling surf roll up and over the beach, over huts, palm trees, the children's dusty football pitch, parked trucks, hotel staff on their way to the first shift, fishermen working on boats, tourists jogging along the shore. All people and most things were swept away and there was nothing to be heard above the roar of the ocean.

The sea mounted the land in a way Brendan wouldn't have thought possible. He stumbled upwards, clawing his way between prickly bushes and tangled undergrowth, pulling himself from one tree trunk to the next.

Maya's ramshackle bus was swept away and she drowned, like all of the passengers except the youngest. Lily was torn out of her arms and somehow, miraculously, tossed into the arms of a tall tree where she lodged until the water subsided.

He never relaxed. For two years after the tsunami, he worked night and day helping survivors to rebuild their homes. Now he was trying to rebuild his business, which might also provide employment for others. What had happened tied him to this place. He didn't have the heart to leave. He was working towards providing a home for Lily as her grandparents, who were also survivors, were now old.

So today, like every day, Brendan rehearsed what he could do in the time left to him, how he could best use the remaining minutes and days of his life.

He slipped on his flip-flops and walked to the seashore for his first check of the day.

At the Launderette

Carole had just put two loads of washing on when the boy slouched in through the launderette door, a plastic sack slung over his shoulder. He sat down awkwardly in an orange chair and stared at the machines. He tugged his black hood down over his forehead.

There were just the two of them in the room. The attendant was in the cubby-hole at the back, eating her sandwiches and reading a newspaper.

The youth didn't seem in any hurry to do his washing. What was he waiting for?

From where she was sitting, Carole could see little of his face, but his hunched body, ripped denims, looped chains and dirty trainers said to her, 'Keep away, I'm nasty, I'm trouble.'

Don't worry, Carole thought, I won't be going anywhere near you. She moved to the other end of the row of chairs and wrote a 'to pack' list.

Perhaps it hadn't been such a brilliant idea to come to the launderette, the sort of place she hadn't stepped into since she was a student, but their machine at home was broken and they were off on holiday the next day.

'Just take the clothes dirty,' Adrian had said as she stuffed shirts, socks, pyjamas, bras and pants into bags. 'Pete and Laura are sure to have a washing machine.'

'Adrian,' she'd shrieked, 'we're not going all the way to Australia with suitcases of dirty washing. What sort of first impression would that make with Laura?' First impressions were so important.

'I see what you mean,' he'd agreed soothingly, and had driven her to the launderette.

What with their son Peter's emigration to the other side of the world, his new relationship, and the prospect of a long-haul flight, she was about as stressed as she could be.

But then she did have to speak to the hooded youth. As she piled her husband's clothes into the dryer, she realised one of his cotton socks was missing, probably flattened against the inside of the washing machine. This was the washer that the youth was now opening for his clothes, having sat silently in the chair for half an hour.

'Excuse me,' Carole said, 'I think—' He turned towards her, his mouth set in a thin line. His green eyes stared out at her from under the black hood as if he had never before seen a middle-aged woman in sweater, skirt and lilac anorak. 'Somewhere in there might be a sock.' She felt herself go beetroot as she fished around in the drum. He was watching her as she retrieved Adrian's beige sock. 'Thanks.'

He waited until she went over to the dryers. Then he opened his dustbin bag up very close to the machine. He seemed to be piling in his washing furtively so that she couldn't see the garments, even if she wanted to.

Suddenly, he was standing in front of her. 'Got any change?' He was standing rigidly in front of her, holding out his hand. His manner seemed threatening.

'Y-yes, maybe.' Oh no, her handbag was out of reach on a far chair and what's more, gaping open, asking to be rifled through or snatched. She was relieved to see the wallet still there. 'How much would you like?'

He pulled a torn fiver out of his pocket. 'Cheers,' he mumbled when she handed him the coins. Each of his knuckles sported a tattoo. His fingernails were bitten right down, the cuticles ragged and red.

He put his wash on the hottest setting and then slumped back down into the chair, head bowed, hands fidgeting.

Carole couldn't help thinking of all the reasons why someone might bring clothes and put them on the ninety degree wash in the launderette. To remove mud, finger-prints, hair… bloodstains.

The attendant was still round the back, but presumably, if anything bad happened, she'd come out to help.

It was freezing. Carole walked over to shut the door and as she passed the washers she glanced at his clothes sloshing around in the suds. All the garments were white.

Her dryer had stopped. It had definitely stopped working. She put her head around the cubby-hole door to ask for help but the attendant was asleep, snoring, feet up on the table. She didn't like to disturb her.

Carole watched the hoody take his washing out of the machine. She watched him tenderly scoop up each item, hold it to the light, shake it softly as if it was gossamer, or finest silk, not just plain cotton. Then he folded each and placed it in the basket.

'Seen enough?' he snapped.

'Baby clothes,' she gasped. Then because she realised that sounded odd, she quickly added, 'What lovely, white baby clothes.'

'Lovely, white, yes,' he repeated as if considering her words carefully. He pushed his hood back to reveal hair that grew only patchily over his scalp.

'You have a baby?' She knew it was very nosy of her to ask.

'Had a baby,' he replied. He lugged the washing basket over to the dryers. He looked incredibly young.

'I, I didn't mean to—'

'It's OK, I'm used to it,' he said tolerantly. 'You've got to thump that machine to restart it.' Carole did as he advised and then he continued, 'She was ill when she was born and then she got a virus and that was that.' He piled the nighties and babygros into a dryer. 'I'm washing them for the last time, then I'll take them to the charity shop. It's hard but I've got to.'

'Why don't you keep them? You could have another baby.'

He shook his head. 'Nah. Just seeing her little clothes cuts me and my girlfriend up. We can't keep them.' She thought he was going to cry.

She wanted to put her arms around him, wanted to look after him as if he were her own son, but what she said was, 'I'm sorry. I'm terribly sorry.' He smiled sadly and they stood there, side by side, waiting for the washing to dry.

A Taste of Honey

They'd been to the holiday cottage before and knew its pluses and minuses. A big plus was that it was virtually free.

'*Tasting much sweeter than wine...*'

A song murmured away, a song from a time when going to the beach just meant picking up a bikini and a tiny towel and setting out.

She was driving three kids: eight, six and a grizzling ten-month-old. 'Stop squabbling, Alice, Joe, Tally. Look out for the sea.' She opened the window and a family of flies zoomed in plus a strong aroma of countryside.

'There, look, look!' Joe said optimistically.

'That's hills, dumbo,' Alice said.

'Mum, Mum, it's the sea, isn't it, Mum?'

At home, she was always Mum now, never Sasha.

The cottage was on its own at the end of a long bumpy track, had a tumbledown barn to one side, and a front door that stuck on the uneven floor and needed to be shoved open or shut.

One day they'd all stay in a villa with sparkling tiled

floors, a pool and a view. 'They'd all' meant something different this July than it had the same time last year.

When they arrived, the two older ones galloped straight upstairs and Joe said, 'Mum there's creepy-crawlies, noisy ones, in the loo.'

'It's a bee, you idiot,' Alice said, rolling her eyes.

The stairs were steep and creaking, the ceilings low as cottage ceilings are, and the dusty sitting room looked as if all the unwanted gifts collected during a long marriage had been deposited randomly around it.

Sasha unpacked the groceries. Seven nights, that was all.

There were several dozy bees stuck to the kitchen curtains so she used a spatula to prise them off, catching them in a sieve and then chucking them out of the window.

It was a cob cottage with eaves that martins nested in, and doors that frogs could squeeze under so she wasn't surprised by an infestation of bugs.

'Kids,' she called, 'a quick tea and then down to the beach.' She was trying to be holiday-ish. The smell of mould, bones, cobwebs and sewage was no different from last year, so sea-breezes would be welcome.

Joe came in from the garden with a huge bunch of wilting plants. 'Mum, are these proper flowers?'

She took the buttercups, dandelions and fragile love-in-a-mists. 'Of course, they're proper flowers, Joe. Thank you.'

Alice arranged them in an old jar with a torn label they'd found in the cupboard. She read out painstakingly, 'Pure Devon Honey…prod…uced by Leo Cobble – that's a funny name, Mum, isn't it? – Cobbleditch'.

The beach, snugly enclosed by cliffs, was in shadow by the time they arrived. It was empty apart from themselves and one lone dog walker with a mobile clamped to his ear.

Alice and Joe raced off to the rock pools near the sea and she dragged the buggy backwards, making deep ridges in the smooth, damp sand. She parked, gently eased Tally's drooping head into a more comfortable sleeping position, then sat down on her fleece, and admired the view. Pale grey sky, a milky sun sinking down to the horizon, a stretch of sea, waves tumbling relentlessly onto the curve of the shore.

I'm on my own now. I'm on my own now. She would learn what that meant, would convince herself of the fact if she persevered. She was like millions of other women.

Except she wasn't like millions of other women, and she didn't know how to deal with it.

Also, she wasn't on her own. She had the children. All the time.

'Mum, Mum, look at this!' Joe trailed a swathe of greeny-brown bladderwrack up the beach.

Alice had collected a bucket of shells, tiny yellow ones, razors and limpets.

'Let's leave these behind, shall we?' Sasha said, feeling mean. She couldn't face the inevitable handicraft session that Alice would insist on: gluing shells to cardboard, tin, bits of wood, making early Christmas presents.

She had always been the practical one, Paul the artist and dreamer. On her own she could just about get the children away on holiday, do the picnics, the washing, the shopping. She couldn't do the artwork.

He had left her in the lurch with three children. She couldn't communicate with him. She had tried but it didn't work and so she'd given up. It was nearly six months now.

They left the beach and drove back along narrow, high-hedged lanes.

She sensed there was something amiss as soon as they'd bumped over the grassy yard and parked at the front of the cottage. There was a stillness about the place, a quietness, except for…?

She clasped an arm around each child and left Tally asleep in her car seat.

Joe wriggled free, put his tiny shoulder to the door but couldn't open it.

'Let me do it – you stay here,' she said.

Inside, all was dark. She couldn't see anything because the daylight from outside was somehow blocked. She moved along the hall to the living room. The place was murmuring something. Humming. The cottage was chanting.

She switched on the light and screamed. The unshaded beam picked outlines, circles, hanging clumps, all black, swaying, moving just a little. Creeping up the walls, crawling over the ceiling, clinging to the ragged velvet curtains.

There was a funny, slightly sweet smell.

'Out, out!' She grabbed Alice who had come in with her, pushing her into the garden.

She heaved the door shut.

'What is it, Mum?' Alice whispered, her face screwed up with worry. Joe started sobbing.

'Listen, you must not go back in there, do you hear me?' she said. 'It's bees. Thousands of them, all over the place.'

Under certain terrible circumstances, even one bee sting could kill you. She remembered a holiday in Greece when a man sitting at the table next to them amongst the profusion of oleanders had been stung and had died within an hour.

The suddenness had been shocking.

'Poor man. When your time's up, that's it. But, Sasha, our time's not up,' Paul had reassured her. 'We're fine. We're fine.'

She couldn't say they'd been blissfully happy, just normally happy, with ordinary problems. No truly serious problems, though. If only she'd realised that before.

But even if she had realised it, it would have made no difference. Paul would still have had the accident, knocked over as he crossed the road just before four p.m., listening to Dylan on his iPod.

If only she'd warned him not to do that when he'd set out that day. If only.

'Mum, Mum,' Alice pleaded, tugging at her sweater, 'don't just stand there. Get the bees out.'

'I can't, darling,' she replied. She should be able to sort the problem out but she couldn't. She felt helpless. 'The bees are swarming. Just let me think a moment. I'll think of what to do.'

Would they swarm and then fly off? She thought not. The sun had gone down. It was late. There had to be a solution.

'I want to go home,' Joe whined.

She could not drive them all back to London. She'd fall asleep at the wheel. In spite of all her earlier resolves, she allowed herself to think, if only Paul was with us, this would be all right.

She had decided early on as he lay completely oblivious to them all, wrapped in bandages, plastered and wired up, that she would never, ever allow herself to dwell on 'if only'.

But sometimes, like now, she couldn't help it.

If Paul was with them, they would get in the car and

drive off home, or to a small hotel, or to the police station which they would be able to find together quite easily.

But he was never going to leave the hospital alive. It had simply been too long. Too long since he had listened to anybody or said anything.

The first three months she had sat by his bed for most of every day and many nights. She'd brought the children to see him regularly for short visits.

But then she'd got exhausted, demoralised.

Her mobile was unfortunately in the cottage and probably submerged by bees.

She drove them all back along the road towards the sea. Somewhere she'd seen a pub.

The bar-lady was sympathetic but they had no available rooms that night. She said that Sasha could use their phone to ring the emergency services, the Police or Fire Service.

She hesitated, feeling awkward about calling bees an emergency.

'What you need, my darling, is a beekeeper,' a woman drinking at the bar said. 'To get them little buggers into a hive.'

'You're so right,' Sasha agreed. But nobody in the pub knew of a beekeeper.

She remembered there was a name on the old jar they'd used for Joe's flowers. That person would know of a bee-keeper, might even be one himself. What was he called? Her mind went blank.

'Alice, can you remember the name?' she asked, handing her and Joe a packet of crisps each.

Alice said, 'Of course I remember it, Mum.' As if it was obvious that she would.

By some miracle, when Sasha had found out his number

in the phone directory and called him from the pub, Leo Cobbleditch was at home, and was a beekeeper. Although at first he didn't want to set out at ten p.m., and drive fifteen miles each way, the prospect of a free swarm was sufficient motivation.

Leo Cobbleditch was an elderly man wearing yellow cord trousers, check shirt, a beekeeper's hat and veil and a pair of leather gloves. These garments, a brush, a cotton sheet and a large cardboard box were all he seemed to need for the job.

'They don't mean no harm, they'm with their queen, so us's got to find her. When she's in the box, I reckon they'll follow.'

After a few minutes, he beckoned Sasha to the door.

'They'm wonderful little fellows, bees, little treasures. They just keep going, whatever life throws at them.'

He wandered around, tapping bees into the box. 'They like conversation. You must always tell bees any family news. They don't take kindly to being left out. Do ye?' he whispered.

She stood in the hall, watching, listening to Leo's gentle talk, and the bees' buzzings as they circled the living room then flew in a line and poured into the cardboard box with the queen. 'I'll search the house and collect up the stragglers,' Leo said, folding the lid over securely. 'They do say it's unlucky if a bee flies into your house and straight out again. That's why my missus always keeps flowers indoors. Encourages 'em to stay.'

'I'm due for a load of good luck, then,' Sasha said.

'I should say so. I reckon you've got near on ten thousand in here. A pretty good swarm, particularly for July.'

She felt incredibly relieved.

He thought he'd got them all, but advised her to check

the bedrooms before they went to sleep. He was delighted with his swarm.

When Sasha waved him off, she glanced up and was surprised to see a canopy of stars, fairy tale bright.

Inside the cottage, all was quiet, all calm. She found a forgotten bee resting on a book in the hall so she carried it outside. As the bee flew away, she willed this lone messenger to take her wishes to Paul. A bit fanciful, maybe, but why not? Her children were forever making wishes. She put the three of them to bed, then went herself. She had coped with the day.

Her dreams were busy, crowded with doctors, traffic, flying insects, stormy seas, missing children. She was being pursued by bees. She was in a film. The noise was horrendous. She awoke sweating and trembling. Her mobile was ringing but it was out of reach.

The hospital had left a message, asking her to contact them.

When she rang back, the nurse said that the previous night Paul had become agitated, had tried to sit up, had called out for something or someone, before slipping back again. They thought Sasha ought to know that his condition might be changing although they couldn't be sure, and it was very early days.

People did emerge from long comas, Sasha knew that, but it was unusual after six months. They'd told her his brain was damaged. But brains could repair themselves, find new pathways.

'Mum, that man makes ornaments out of shells,' Alice said. 'He's going to give us some if we go to his cottage.'

'This afternoon we'll go to tea with that nice beekeeper man and his wife, as they've invited us,' Sasha said. 'And then, we'll go home.'

'Mum!' Alice shrieked. 'All that trouble with the bees and now you're taking us home before we've even had our holiday! Why?'

'I think Daddy's missing us, that's why. We need to get back to see him, talk to him. Tell him our news.'

'That's like what Mr Cobboldewitch said about the bees,' said Joe. 'They like people telling them things.'

Sasha hugged her three children together and then started to repack the car.

Swimming with Turtles

The plastic handles on the shopping bags cut into Julie's hands as she hurried back to her car in the town square. Although only four p.m., it was getting dark. Her hair was dripping, her mac sodden and she was frozen. She'd left her ten-year-old daughter Katy, who was still recovering from leukaemia, with their next-door neighbour.

The lights from the travel shop reflected in ripples across the puddles and attracted her attention to the display in the window advertising bargain breaks. There were last-minute sunshine holidays to Tenerife, Madeira, Morocco and the Caribbean. The holidays were half price or less but, she reminded herself, there were more important things to spend her money on, weren't there?

As she drove home, a little voice in her head said, 'You both need some sunshine. Have some fun now – who knows what the future will bring?'

She mentioned the idea to her friend Doreen as they had a cup of tea. 'I thought you didn't like flying, Julie,' Doreen said.

Julie nodded ruefully. She remembered only too well her panic last time she'd got on a plane and all the upset it had caused. It had ruined their week in Spain as she'd dreaded the thought of the return flight. Her behaviour hadn't gone down at all well with Mark who expected everything in their lives to run like clockwork.

If only she'd been a different sort of person, or he had, they might not have split up, she thought.

Doreen smiled sympathetically, 'You and Katy have been through a lot in the last year, Julie. Maybe keep things simple. Go to your Mum's caravan, as usual.'

But Julie couldn't get the holiday idea out of her head. It was about sunshine, going somewhere completely new, giving her life the kickstart it needed, giving Katy some carefree days.

When she mentioned it to her mother on the phone that evening, her mother said, 'You could both do with a break but it would use up most of the money Grandad left you. I thought you were keeping it for a rainy day.'

'This is a rainy day, Mum.' In every sense, Julie thought.

Katy had been ill for eighteen months and would need more treatment, according to the doctors. But a holiday could only do good. Julie could save the nest egg for their future but recently the here-and-now had become more pressing.

'Go on, Mum, it would be fabulous. Can I have time off school?' Julie smiled at her daughter's thin face and sparkly green eyes. 'Are there sharks? Can I swim in the sea, or is it an ocean?' Katy asked, flapping the brochure under Julie's nose. 'I want to see dolphins and turtles.'

'So, that's it then,' Julie's mother said, 'going all that way to see turtles you could look at just as well in the aquarium in town.' Then, when she saw Katy's face, her manner softened. 'Go on both of you, it's the chance of a lifetime.

We've practically turned into fish ourselves with all this rain.'

'Perhaps you'll meet someone nice,' Doreen suggested. That was an appealing thought. It was quite a while since Mark had announced he'd had enough of hospital waiting rooms, chemotherapy side-effects, and arguments. He was as unhappy as she was about Katy, he'd explained, but he needed to have a life of his own, too.

Julie's shock at hearing this had been followed by relief – no more terrible rows, no more trying to placate her husband. She could concentrate on Katy.

Recently she'd become incredibly angry whenever she thought about him. How could he walk out on them both at such a time? When he rang, she just handed the phone straight to Katy.

Julie took eye patches, Bach flower remedies, an inflatable neck rest, a *Vanquish your Fears* self-help book and a bag of boiled fruit sweets to help her through the flight. Surprisingly, she settled down quite easily in the plane. It was probably because she had a purpose in going. And Katy's enthusiasm was infectious.

Their apartment in Barbados was only a few rows back from the shore.

It was the fourth day of their week and they knew how to work the shower so it didn't scald them, which was the best palm tree to sit under and which beach café served the crispiest French fries.

'Mum, don't forget your mask and flippers!' Katy shouted as she grabbed her beach bag, ran out of the door and along the sandy path leading to the shore. She was so excited and her energy levels had improved which was wonderful.

'Put your hat on,' Julie called, running after her daughter to the small boat moored by the rocks. The sun's rays were powerful and Katy's hair was still just a thin layer of down.

There were eight of them on the boat: Jim, the boatman, a couple who had eyes only for each other, and a man with his two young sons.

'There are only three things to remember,' Jim said as he increased the throttle and swung his boat out to sea. 'Don't chase the turtles. Don't try to ride on their backs and,' he smiled at Katy, who looked even whiter against his dark skin, 'have FUN!'

The day was beyond perfect: blue sky, clear, calm sea, light breeze, a sun that caressed their bare arms and legs, relaxing all the winter's tension.

Jim said they had a twenty-minute ride along the coast to the spot where the turtles liked to swim. As they chugged along he pointed out landmarks. 'That's where Rihanna lives – you know, she was born on the island. Cliff spends the winters here in his fabulous house. If you're lucky, you might even see Prince Harry here on holiday.' Amusing, gentle chat, that didn't require a reply.

'Turtles are very clever,' Jim continued, talking especially to the three children on board. 'They know just when this little boat will put down anchor in Pelican Bay.'

Katy grinned from underneath her hat at the two boys sitting opposite her. It was ages since she'd mixed with other kids. The younger boy smiled back, the older one scowled, concentrating on cleaning his goggles and snorkel tube. 'Where's the camera, Dad?' he asked his father who unclipped a transparent plastic box from his belt and checked it.

'Won't that get wet?' Katy asked.

'It's an underwater camera,' the younger boy replied.

'Dad's going to let me use it,' his brother added.

'No, Ben, I'm not,' his father replied firmly.

'You promised, Dad,' Ben argued trying to snatch it from his father.

'Ben, I explained before we set out. I can't risk the camera getting dropped to the seabed. We'd never find it.' The man ran his hands through his curly dark hair, an exasperated expression on his face. 'Your mother asked me to take photos of you and Luke and that's what I'll do,' he said, slinging the camera around his neck.

'Hey, guys!' Jim called, switching the engine off now they were at the right spot. 'You wanna watch me feed the turtles?' He scooped a handful of crumbs from a metal canister and threw them onto the water. The two boys and Katy scrambled to the back of the boat to wait and watch for turtles.

'The two of them really keep me on my toes,' the man remarked to Julie.

'It's a wonderful place for kids to let off steam, isn't it? With all the outdoor activities,' Julie said.

'Fantastic,' he agreed. 'I don't see enough of my boys so when I do it can take a while for us to shake down together. Know what I mean?'

Julie nodded. 'My daughter's been through such a lot.' She startled herself by saying this. She didn't usually confide in strangers but there was something sweet about this man.

'Has she been unwell? She looks such a livewire.' He glanced at his sons who were counting the turtles, now just below the surface of the sea. 'I'd be devastated if either of mine were seriously ill. We men take that sort of thing badly.'

Julie was quiet for a few moments. 'It's true – people do react differently to terrible events. Maybe I need to remember that.' Her thoughts turned to Mark and the angry criticisms she'd slung at him when she'd felt desperate about Katy. She'd accused him of not taking their daughter's illness seriously enough. He'd replied: One of us needs to try and stay calm.

'Don't just sit there, Mum! The turtles are here! See – they're nibbling the food.'

Katy pulled on her flippers and would have been over the side of the boat in a trice if Jim hadn't said, 'Whoa, there, little mermaid, wait for Mama.'

'Stay close to me, Katy.' Julie was worried about sharks, about Katy drifting too far from the boat, maybe getting tangled in seaweed, and being bitten by the turtles.

There were so many awful things that could happen in life, she wondered how she'd had the courage to bring her daughter all this way on holiday. But so far it was a success. Her grandad, whose favourite motto was *carpe diem*, would have approved, she thought. Even though, for himself, he'd never wanted to go anywhere other than Bournemouth.

Julie and Katy linked arms and swam around the boat, above the twenty or so turtles. They ranged in size from small – not much bigger than a dinner plate – to one so huge you probably could ride on its back. They all had beautiful brown and cream shells with subtly different markings and they all had the same way of flipping through the water as if they were flying.

The turtles stayed as a group but well spread out so Julie, Katy, the man with his two sons and the doting couple could swim along without getting in each other's way.

Jim had told them turtles could communicate with each other across hundreds of miles.

Katy stretched down a toe and stroked a shell. She took out her snorkel tube, silver bubbles escaping from her lips, and mouthed, 'Thank you, Mum!' She blew Julie a kiss before replacing the snorkel and whooshing out the seawater.

Some of the turtles were bolder and more inquisitive than

others. You'd probably find out their individual personalities, if you stayed with them long enough, Julie mused.

Down below them, small pointed fish and the occasional pair of larger angelfish glinted amongst the tongues of brown coral.

Memories of Katy in hospital came into Julie's mind and she felt the usual stomach-tightening and sick, dry mouth. But, unusually, these sensations passed away rapidly. Perhaps it was the relaxing support of the water. Or perhaps the presence of the turtles as they swam past, turning their heads from side to side and gazing from hooded eyes with placid, wise expressions. She'd never forget that sight.

The turtles were reminding her to live in the moment; they seemed to be telling her that no amount of worrying would make Katy better.

The thirty minutes passed in a flash and they were throwing their flippers over the side of the boat and pulling themselves up the little rope ladder. 'Dad would love it here,' Katy said.

'Say cheese! Dad, Luke! Jim!' shouted Ben. He'd been allowed the camera at last. Katy watched with interest.

'Put the camera cord round your—' shouted his father as he pulled himself onto the deck. But, too late. As the boat rocked sideways, Ben fumbled and dropped the camera. They all watched as it skidded along the ledge at the side of the boat.

Katy leaped across the boat and grabbed it just as it bounced towards the sea.

'Katy, I think you're gonna be an athlete one day!' called Jim. 'You're so nimble on your feet!'

When they'd dried themselves the man, whose name Julie didn't yet know, said, 'The boys and I wondered if you and your daughter, Katy, would care to join us for dinner tonight? The beach café does great food.'

'Thank you, but – I'm not sure—' Julie was torn. The company would be nice, in one way.

'Mum—' Katy's expression was crestfallen.

'Just dinner,' he said, 'It's OK.' So she agreed, more for Katy's sake than her own.

Over dinner that evening he gave Julie and Katy the amazing photos he'd taken of them swimming amongst the turtles.

'I'd like to take some photos, Mum,' Katy said. She used Julie's mobile phone to snap a picture of their new friends.

Then Ben took the mobile. 'Don't drop it into your Coca-Cola, Ben!' warned his dad, anxious after the afternoon's events. But Ben was on his best behaviour now and took a photo of Julie and Katy sitting by a leafy trellis which sparkled with fairy lights.

'That's lovely, Ben. Thank you, we'll treasure all the photos,' Julie said.

It had been a perfect evening, Julie reflected when she and Katy got back to their apartment.

'I'm going to text Dad that photo of us,' Katy said.

'OK, darling,' Julie replied easily. She didn't feel even a twinge of annoyance. 'I'm sure it will cheer him up to see you looking so happy and well.'

She hoped the photo would go some way towards erasing the sad images Mark must still have of Katy in hospital and that he would see that, for Katy's sake, she had got over her anger with him. She knew Katy had missed her father and would be very pleased to resume contact with him when they got home.

The text reply came onto her phone early next morning as Julie was savouring the peace, remembering their swim with the turtles, watching the sun rise over the turquoise

Caribbean, waiting for Katy to wake up: 'Love you both. Can I meet you at Gatwick on Wednesday?' She felt the familiar butterflies in her stomach. As she drank her coffee, sitting on their little verandah, she realised that the feelings were excitement rather than anxiety. She started to remember the good things about her husband, how they had been a happy family before the terrible shock of their daughter's illness.

Julie decided to ask Katy whether she'd like her dad to meet them at the airport. She was pretty certain that the answer would be 'Yes!'

No one knew what the future would bring. But for now, all was well.

Works of Art

'It's a sculpture,' her husband said, reading a note in the local church newsletter. 'They're asking if we want it in our church.'

'Who's they?' she asked.

'The vicar and a committee.' He smoothed back his thick grey hair which, Claire thought, could do with cutting.

'How do we know whether we want it until we've seen it?'

'Fair point. Apparently, it's been in the side chapel for the whole of August. Now it's gone back to its creator – who is?' He scanned the closely written sheet for this nugget of information. She passed him his glasses. 'There's going to be a vote. They're calling it a referendum. Quite right, too. We should all be allowed to express our opinion.'

He folded the newsletter and handed it to her to put away. She tucked it under a pile of cookbooks and Sunday papers. She was distracted by that choice of word – referendum – reminding her of Brexit, that touchy subject she didn't now like to bring up at home.

'The sculptor is Ivan something,' Michael said. 'Any

chance of lunch?'

Why did she always have to make it? How had he managed all those years before they got together? But asking him to prepare the meal would cause a row. So she started to peel the potatoes.

'I'll give Mum a quick ring while you get on,' he said, 'We need to think about Christmas.'

What was there to think about? They always had his mother to stay. But why couldn't she go to Michael's brother's? Were his four boys so terrible? Claire's dream was a week, maybe even ten days, in Switzerland over the festive period.

The next day, after she'd walked Nattie to school, Claire called into the church. She joined a group of people standing around holding bits of paper as if they were about to vote.

'She's quite a large lady,' said the man in charge of the referendum box. 'We have to ask ourselves, will she really *fit in*?'

'Do you mean she's tall, or what?' Claire said, gazing around at the vast stone arches, wide aisles and high pitched roof. She was imagining where the statue would reside, but space didn't seem to be the problem.

'We had the grandchildren over in August,' an elderly man said. She recognised him as someone who lived on their road, a few doors down. 'So never saw the thing.'

'We were in Cornwall,' the man behind the referendum box said.

'The church is paying twenty thousand pounds for it if it does go ahead,' a woman said, appearing from behind a pillar. She was probably the wife of the man behind the referendum box Claire thought, from the way she grabbed his arm. 'Twenty thousand!'

'Lavinia,' Referendum Man said, 'we must consider all aspects, not just cost.'

'He's an out and out pagan,' her neighbour said. 'Have you read about all those goings-on in St Ives?'

'He's had at least three so-called wives,' Lavinia said.

They agreed it was essential to see the work of art before deciding, so they put their voting sheets back on the pile. Claire, being the youngest and most able-bodied there, offered to drive them to the sculptor's cottage. She'd have to ask Michael for his car as her own was semi-permanently off the road, having failed its MOT.

She disappeared to buy a local paper as it was Monday. The advert outside the newsagents announced there were '373 Jobs Available!' She read the situations vacant section over a coffee in the café by the church. She'd already seen many, but not all, of the advertised jobs online. She'd phone about the doctor's receptionist job, part-time, non-smoking, caring environment, when she got home and could concentrate. She knew she must find proper work because the redundancy payment from her teaching assistant's job wouldn't last much longer. But she was still hoping to have time for her writing. So far, this occupation (a 'hobby', as Michael called it) had only cost her money, rather than earned it. Sometimes she got drawn into a situation because she thought it could give her ideas. But she needed to take notes and actually write, not just store the material in her head.

The next day Claire wore a long, vivid blue dress and green duffel coat – colours that complemented her auburn hair and looked artistic, she hoped. She collected the three people she'd agreed to take to the sculptor's home. They drove out of town along various lanes and then turned into a rutted, muddy track that ran for at least a mile between two flat, empty fields. The ridge in the middle of the track was covered with brambles and occasional sharp boulders. She gripped the steering wheel, didn't chat or listen, and tried not to wreck the car.

Eventually, they saw a clump of trees and some sheds. Claire manoeuvred the car between narrow gateposts and piles of old tyres. There was a cottage. They walked towards it, passing overgrown spinach and scavenging hens. Before they reached the door, the sculptor, Ivan Peters, walked stiffly to greet them. Although old, he still looked good with his tanned face and bushy white beard. He wore a sailor's cap, cotton smock and paint-spattered cords. You could see he was an artist, Claire thought.

'I'm absolutely delighted you've come to see my Madonna. She took two years to create and is very special to me. I want to see her settled and St Ethelred's seems the most fitting home,' Ivan said.

The Madonna was housed behind three dustbins in an open-fronted lean-to shed. They'd walked past without noticing her on their way to the cottage.

'Well, what do you think? Isn't she magnificent?' Ivan said.

She was tall, about seven-feet high with her crown, or well over two metres. Claire remembered how they didn't ever use feet and inches at school. This shapely Madonna was clasping a serious-looking baby with unusually long legs. Was she beautiful or strange? She was both, Claire decided.

'Yes,' murmured Laurence, the Referendum Man. 'Yes, splendid…striking…most unusual.'

'Modern,' said his wife, Lavinia. Then she whispered to Claire, 'He had me worried for a moment: Madonna. No connections, then, to the living Madonna, the one who had all the husbands and partners decades younger?'

Claire whispered back that she didn't think so, but with art, you couldn't always tell.

'Weren't you once a member of the St Ives School?' Claire's neighbour, Gordon, asked Ivan who said he had been, as a very young man.

'It's rather like a Hepworth, or do I mean Henry Moore? And so pink, such a wonderful colour. Did you say it was alabaster?' Lavinia said.

Ivan seemed pleased. He said he had an agent coming down from London to talk about an exhibition. 'So can I count on you to vote for me?' he enthused, shaking everyone's hands firmly. His own hands were rough with long, curved nails.

'Before we go, could we see some of your other work, your pictures?' Claire asked.

They squashed themselves into his tiny studio shed, bending their bodies round the stacks of paintings, trying not to put feet or elbows through the canvasses.

'I must say there's some jolly good stuff here,' Laurence said.

'Do you recognise that scene? It's that little lane going up to the football pitch, and there's a...I think it's a post van. Or...perhaps not,' Claire said.

'Take it home,' Ivan said to her. When she hesitated, he said, 'You're under no obligation. Bring it back in a few days if you don't like it.'

'Well, of course, it's very nice, but—'

'Go on, take it, take it.'

They said goodbye to Ivan and walked back along the path. Claire was carrying the picture in its rough board frame. Her companions were smiling rather more than usual, probably out of relief that they weren't also carrying something. Of course, everyone glanced at the Madonna as they passed, and this time Claire noticed her face. She had a sweet half-smile on her lips, making her seem vulnerable, and knowing.

Claire wrapped the painting in an old picnic blanket she kept in the boot of the car and the group set off for home.

'He's a wily old devil,' Gordon, said. 'I reckon he's got you hooked.' It was true, she hadn't enquired about the price of the picture, but then, she didn't intend to buy it. She just hadn't been able to say no. But she would.

'What do you think about the Madonna?' she asked while trying to drive down one side of the track keeping the car upright.

'Large, overpowering,' said Laurence who was sitting in the front passenger seat. 'That's just between us. Officially, of course, I have to remain impartial.'

'Funny colour and did you notice that crack running down her chin?' Lavinia said.

'Didn't he say that was a natural variation in the materials?' Gordon added.

'All that money should be spent on the poor, helping the homeless, not tarting up the church,' Lavinia said. Claire sort of agreed, but did it have to be one or the other?

'But didn't the vicar say the money had been bequeathed 'for a work of art', so that's what it's got to be spent on,' Gordon said. 'I like the idea of using a local artist, but perhaps not Ivan.'

'It's the thin end of the wedge,' Laurence, said. 'We'll have the church stuffed with 'works of art' in no time. People won't get a look in.'

'He could do with the money, I expect,' Claire said, thinking of the cottage's peeling paintwork and the missing tiles on the roof. Although Ivan was quite well-known, he'd had some troubles so wasn't flush, or so she'd heard.

She was glad to be driving along a proper road now. She'd got the car out of the awful lane with no damage, just covered with mud and dust.

'I think it would be wonderful to have something in the church which celebrates women.' Claire said. 'Men have had quite enough of the limelight, haven't they?' She'd always thought of herself as a feminist at heart, but she hoped she hadn't offended anyone.

When Michael walked through the door that night looking harassed and his work suit crumpled, he said, 'I've rung Mother and she's agreed to come on the train, if we can run her back.'

'What?' Claire had no idea what he was talking about.

'She says, would we like her to make the pudding as usual? And would it be helpful if she prepared the sprouts in advance?'

This was a reference to the Tesco frozen ones they'd had last year. Claire felt hot and panicky at the mere thought of the festive season. 'Mike! It's not even October. Why don't you ask me about my trip out to Ivan Peters' place?' She gave him the edited version.

The evening would have passed off smoothly if Nattie hadn't come downstairs long after she should have been asleep and said, 'What's that...um...picture in my bedroom cupboard? It's stopping me from going to sleep.' Her eyes were red and her long hair matted, which would be a problem in the morning.

Michael looked at it and said it was terrible. 'The perspective's all wrong. I reckon Natalie could have made a better job of that post van. We can't afford to buy nice pictures, let alone this, Claire.'

Next morning, Claire dropped Michael off at work and

then drove out to Ivan's cottage. She parked by the old tyres, opened the car boot and lifted out the picture, which she'd wrapped in brown paper and tied with string, to show she cared.

She crept along the path to the shed, not stopping to look at the statue which would have distracted her. As she placed the parcel on the step, Ivan, with paintbrush in hand, flung open the door from the inside. 'Mystery woman! Gorgeous creature! What's this?'

She handed him the brown parcel. 'Your picture. I'm sorry, it wasn't quite what we wanted.'

'Come in, come in.'

'I'm not sure…'

'I've a shedful of paintings, as you can see. Take your pick.' He heaved out a vast oil painting of a floodlit tiger running across navy blue grass. 'What about this? It will have pride of place in my next exhibition, if I haven't sold it before then. The agent's coming down from London next week.'

'I'm afraid, it just wouldn't work in our small house. I don't know where I'd hang it.' She thought of Nattie and her nightmares.

'Or this?' It was a bowl of fruit, all curves and rich colours, basking by an open window under a strawberry moon. She shook her head. He pulled out a smaller picture in a gold frame. 'This might be what you're seeking.' It was a turquoise and white butterfly and rather beautiful.

'Women are like butterflies,' he mused. 'Fragile, desirable…'

And collected by men to be pinned in glass cases, she thought.

'I've been chasing them all my life…'

'Ivan! Ivan!' A strong voice that must have been his wife's, was calling from the direction of the cottage.

'Time to go.' He thrust the butterfly picture into her arms and said, 'Take it for a few days. Please. See if you like it. No obligation.' He patted her shoulder with a dusty hand. 'Any news about the church referendum?'

'They're still voting,' she said. 'We'll know at the weekend.'

She walked back to the car with a heavy heart. As she passed the Madonna, she fancied the statue stamped her foot and cast her a disapproving look, as if shouting, Say what you mean and stick to it! There was nothing fragile and butterfly-like about this pink lady.

I will! I will! I most definitely will! That was the very last time any man, any person, was going to wrap her round their little finger. Claire promised.

She'd return the picture on Saturday. Perhaps Michael would help her, but that would mean telling him.

When she got home, Gordon phoned. 'Have you seen today's newspaper? That Lavinia Bottomley has been tweeting like mad about the Madonna. The Echo's picked it up and it's front page news. Jolly bad timing. It'll influence the voting.'

'Oh dear,' Claire said. 'What does she say?'

He started reading: 'The statue is a waste of church money. When so many young people are unemployed and homeless we need to question our consciences before voting yes. The statue is more secular than religious, as shown by the Madonna's crown, and when have we ever seen Ivan Peters in our Church? It has come to something... blah, blah...'

'That's quite a few tweets,' Claire mused.

'They've embroidered her words, you know what they're like,' he said.

'I voted this morning,' Claire said. 'I'm in favour of having it, on balance.' She was glad her husband wasn't home and listening to this as she suspected he'd voted against it. She didn't want another Brexit referendum argument, not after the rows they'd had a couple of years ago. She'd nearly had to consult a counsellor about their marriage.

'I'm for it, too,' he said. 'There's no doubt Ivan could do with the money. He's a real character and not a bad artist either, but all that talk about agents coming down from London is just wishful thinking, I'm afraid.'

She told him the story of the pictures and he laughed. 'I told you he was a wily old fellow. It takes one to know one.'

While Nattie ate her tea in front of the TV, Claire showed her the butterfly picture. 'It's our little secret,' she said. 'Just for a few days, then I'm taking it back to the artist.'

'OK, Mum.'

She didn't dare tell Michael. Instead, to cheer him up, she mentioned how she'd got an interview at the surgery.

'Good.' Then he frowned. 'But Claire, what about a proper job, using your teaching skills?' He meant full-time. But they'd come to parenthood later in life and Claire wanted to have time and energy for Nattie, so she'd rather do part-time, if they could manage.

'Have you voted in the referendum?' she asked, then wanted to bite back her words.

'I'm abstaining. It's all got too political.'

The next evening Claire went for an interview at the surgery and was offered the job. She said she'd let them know. Would it be enough work? Walking home through the town she bumped into Laurence.

'We've just done the count and it's a clear no,' he said. 'The opposite of what we expected.'

'What a shame. Ivan's going to be terribly upset.'

'It was never suitable for our church. But the churchwardens are embarrassed, having encouraged him. You wouldn't mind phoning Ivan to explain, would you? It would come so much better from you. He likes you.'

Claire didn't have a good track record of refusing requests like that. A vision of the Madonna with an imperious expression on her face and standing seven-foot tall in her bare feet flashed before her eyes. 'No, I'm sorry. *No*, absolutely not my role,' she said, as firmly as possible. He looked momentarily crestfallen. She didn't waver.

When she got home she phoned the surgery and accepted the job. They asked her to start the next day as several receptionists were off with flu.

'I'm afraid my first month's pay will go on this picture,' she said to her husband that evening, producing the butterfly from the kitchen cupboard. She'd never before bought a painting, or indeed anything major for the house, without consulting him first. The butterfly was a gorgeous turquoise reminder of recent events, also a warning. Don't be a butterfly, Claire resolved.

'I see. I suppose you felt Ivan needed the money?'

'Yes. I think he was relying on the church taking the Madonna.'

'Mmm.' He seemed bemused.

'The surgery wants me to do extra hours over Christmas, and I'd like to. They're opening a special clinic for homeless people. It means we won't be able to have Mother this year, I'm sorry.'

'She wouldn't mind you working on Christmas Day,' he said. 'We could have dinner in the evening.'

'Only if you cook it.'

'I see.' He looked down at his cottage pie thoughtfully. 'Maybe she would prefer it at my brother's. She could get to know the boys better.'

'Does that mean I can watch what I want on TV at Christmas?' asked Nattie, grinning like a Cheshire cat.

'Yes,' said Michael. 'Within reason.'

In November, Claire received a phone call from someone who said he was Ivan Peters' agent. He said he wanted her to return the butterfly oil painting as it was part of a set and they needed it for the London exhibition. He already had a potential buyer.

Claire was startled by the unexpected call and, to give herself time to think, she asked if he knew what had happened to the Madonna.

'Oh, that.' The agent sighed impatiently. 'It's caused a tricky situation. Ivan offered it to two churches in Wiltshire. They've both agreed to buy it and neither will back off. They simply love it. Of course, *entre nous*, they've spotted a bargain. With church funds as they are these days, who can blame them?'

'It is rather a lovely work of art,' she agreed.

'Now,' the agent said, a harder note to his voice. 'What about the butterfly oil? I don't think Ivan ever intended to break up his set. Rather a mistake, I'm afraid, but he is getting on a bit, as you know. I hope you'll play fair with him.'

She knew Ivan had cashed the cheque she'd sent him at the end of her first month's work at the surgery.

'I bought the picture from the artist himself and there's quite a story attached,' she replied. 'It means a lot to me and I don't know if I could possibly part with it.'

She was ready to stand firm, and then, finally, to negotiate. A two-week holiday in a five-star hotel in Switzerland didn't come cheap, even if they weren't going for Christmas. Christmas would be, at last, just the three of them, at home.

Roses

It had rained continuously, one of those days that never really gets light. Harry searched through the bins and found a pack of crayfish sandwiches, only just out of its date, some mushy bananas and a flabby pizza.

He settled down, sleeping bag rolled by his side, carrier bag tucked into the small of his back. It was too early to go to St Peter's hostel. Best not to arrive before nine-thirty. Slip straight into the bunk, avoid meaningless chat.

He pulled up the hood on his threadbare anorak and leant back out of the rain. When queues formed outside the restaurants, he ambled over, 'Spare us a few bob for the night, enough for a cuppa, need to catch a bus to the night-shelter.' He was rather ashamed of his beggar's voice – the result of decades on the streets.

A youngish couple whisked past. 'Don't stop, Tania, they're all the same,' the man said.

'Darling, we can give something,' Tania said, flicking back her glossy hair and tugging at her man's arm. He rustled through his pockets. Harry waited, trying to look humble. Eventually, Tania found a fifty pence piece in her evening bag.

He collected more money in this way and felt satisfied, even though he was sodden right through. He'd buy himself a proper coat at the charity shop tomorrow.

From where he was now sitting, Harry had a view through the restaurant window. He could see Tania and her man, in the candlelight. The man ordered another bottle of wine. Then he bought a rose from the seller who, Harry knew, could sometimes get £10 for a single bloom. Tania took it and tucked it behind her ear.

Next time Harry looked, the couple were arguing. The man glowered at the waiter, paid the bill and they left. Harry pulled himself back into the office doorway.

'I'm so embarrassed,' Tania shouted. 'Complaining about every course, not leaving a tip, spoiling our evening.'

'I bought you a rose, didn't I? What more do you want?'

Tania chucked the rose into the gutter near Harry's feet. 'Two dozen roses, not just one, Mr Skinflint.'

The rose lay in the drab gutter under the street lamp, raindrops sparkling like diamonds on its glowing red petals. It looked so beautiful Harry was minded to pick it up, but what would he do with it? And he could just hear the taunts he'd get at St Peter's if he arrived with a poncy rose.

The flower reminded him of his nan. Didn't she grow roses in the front garden? Harry pictured himself as a little lad helping her feed their roots, water and prune them. Ouch! He remembered the thorns. In his mind's eye, he buried his face into their enormous dewy heads, could feel their cool silkiness against his skin, smell their perfume.

His mum had inherited Nan's love of roses. She'd kept a crumbling spray in a box at the bottom of her wardrobe, a reminder of her wedding day. It had stayed there even though Harry's dad had proved to be a far from perfect husband. Mum was a kind, generous person.

He might have been able to return once Dad had died if he'd kept in touch as a son should. But he'd never been back to Eskdale Villas, not since that day when he'd been unable to tell his parents that he'd got the sack, yet again. He'd neglected his mother for so long she'd not want to see him now. She wouldn't recognise him.

It didn't do to dwell on the past, though. He had to keep positive to get through each day.

Even so, he couldn't leave the rose to get trampled on by uncaring feet. He rescued it and stowed it in his bag.

As Harry trudged up the hill to the shelter, the idea came to him that he would buy one of those padded envelopes and send the dewy, perfect rose to Mum. He hoped it would touch her heart.

Next morning, as he munched cornflakes and drank a mug of weak tea, Harry unwrapped the flower from its newspaper protection.

Of course, it was dead, the petals ragged and bruised.

He'd been mad to think it would last overnight without water. Like everything else in his life, it had disintegrated. Harry broke its stalk, scooped the petals off the table and chucked the whole lot in the bin.

'You all right?' asked a young bloke with dreadlocks.

'Yeah, mate, fantastic,' Harry replied. It had been a big thing, planning to send the rose to Mum, and he'd been thwarted. Typical.

But, somehow, Harry couldn't abandon his idea.

'I hope you are well,' he wrote on the postcard. On the reverse was a stunning photograph of the town's rose garden. 'These roses reminded me of you. I'm at the hostel.'

His hands were stiff and his handwriting enormous, so that was all he could fit on it, along with his mother's name and address. The card and postage were costly but he didn't begrudge it. Sending it, trying to make contact with her, eased his mind.

Of course, he didn't hear anything back.

'You can't trust the post these days,' he grumbled over breakfast then wished he hadn't. He felt stupid – he hadn't given a proper address, hadn't really considered that his mother would now be well over eighty.

'Post?' the dreadlocks bloke said. 'What's that?' Then he paused, his expression softening. 'Your Mum's maybe moved, maybe she's…'

Harry knew what the bloke meant. But he was sick of conversation.

Three weeks later, as he settled under the pier for the night, Dreadlocks approached him. 'Your name Harry?'

'Why?'

'They're looking for you at St Peter's. They've been asking round town for you. Your Mum's in a home. Wants to see you.'

'Thanks, mate, thanks,' Harry said, his heart lurching and pounding. He picked up his few belongings, shook the sand off and set off up the hill to the night shelter.

Night Zoo

'I always get hyenas and jackals muddled up,' she said. 'I think hyenas are noisier though, aren't they?' He didn't answer, whether it was because he was too tired, or just hadn't heard (he was quite deaf now), she didn't know.

It was surprisingly restful to sit on the rickety little train and be conveyed along a meandering track past indigo bushes, palm trees, streams and occasional animal shapes that were mostly silent and stationary. But you knew they were there. The train was small-scale, slow and open-sided like the ones that drive along beach promenades back home. A train for children, really, but they were mainly adults on this trip around the Night Zoo.

It was the end of summer in Singapore, and the air was full of moisture though now there was a chilly edge to the warm breeze. Two animals hulked under some tropical trees, their horns pale in the moonlight.

'I get rhinos and hippos muddled up, too,' she continued.

'They are quite similar, so I can understand that, Beverley,' her husband replied, yawning, taking a packet of peanuts from his pocket and making it clear that he was there under sufferance. He'd said all along there wasn't time for this excursion. He'd wanted to rest in their hotel until they went to the airport for their night flight to Brisbane.

'I shouldn't eat those,' she said. 'You can't possibly be hungry after all that buffet food. And we're getting another meal after this!'

Mealtimes were topsy-turvy and their body clocks would only get more out of kilter as they did the next stretch of their journey.

She supposed she loved him. But he had rather slowed down and had some irritating ways. Now he was looking sulky about her peanuts warning.

'I'm sorry, Si,' she said. 'You're tired and I know you didn't want to come on this.' Why was she always the one who said sorry in their relationship?

She allowed jet lag to take over, didn't fight it, didn't try to unscramble hyena from jackal, both predatory and sly, or hippo from rhino, both large and thick-skinned. To her, the animals of each pair had always been similar, ever since she'd read about them in her old set of *Children's Encyclopedias*.

Which was more dangerous? She forgot almost as soon as the Singaporean guide at the front of the train told them. One of them could charge faster than a person could run, so you'd stand no chance. But none of the animals in this Night Zoo were a threat to their visitors, that's what they were told. The different species were safely separated from each other, and people, by deep ditches. It was much more humane than cages and bars.

Were hyenas, jackals and dingos all much the same? She started thinking about that dingo baby case years ago in the Outback.

It was odd how jet lag affected her. Alert one moment, the next her head lolling sideways onto Simon's shoulder, her thoughts looping together so she couldn't remember the simplest facts that the whispering guide told them. At the same time, people and events from way back swam into her mind with unexpected clarity.

'Do you remember when you were in that band – what was it called?'

He didn't answer. He was looking out for mouse-deer, no bigger than cats. They were so tiny they were probably hiding under leaves.

Now they'd reached the hyena section. Or were they jackals? She peered into the darkness, trying to catch a sense of their outlines, their backs and legs against the scrub.

As she pushed her arm into a sleeve of her cardigan, she heard something metal tinkle to the ground, whatever it was falling onto the track. She thought it was a button, which was a nuisance as her cashmere cardigan was special, and she was planning to wear it as part of her outfit for Juno's wedding.

'Simon, did you hear that clink back there? Something fell over the side. I'm sorry.' He didn't reply so she assumed he hadn't heard. Never mind, it was unimportant.

'Was it Foxy something? Or something Foxes?' she continued, referring to his band. In those days Simon had been thin and fast-talking. Quite funny, too. Girls swarmed round him. She'd read somewhere recently that the number one quality women looked for in a man was a sense of humour. He'd certainly had that.

'Do you remember how Philippa used to bake all those cakes, working her way right through the recipe book: angel cake, Battenburg, chocolate, coffee, date, eclairs, fruit and… staying up late at night, you'd have thought she was—'

'*Shsh!*' he hissed. 'They told us to keep quiet. Don't scare the animals.'

They had been given various pieces of advice at the start of their circuit of the zoo. One of the instructions was not to take photos as the flash could blind these nocturnal animals. So their digital camera was packed away. She predicted that it would not be used until they got to the wedding. No doubt Simon would then take umpteen photos. He'd always had a bit of a thing for Philippa and even though they'd never met her daughter, Juno, he'd insisted they must accept the invitation.

It had been very odd, she remembered, the way Philly had left university so abruptly midway through and hared off to Oz with somebody she'd hardly known five minutes.

It hadn't really seemed to fit with the cake baking, because Australia was all barbies and surfing, wasn't it?

'Simon, sorry but don't drop peanuts over the side – we mustn't feed them or they will get too close, and they might attack. That's what they said.'

In no time, Philly had three or four kids and Christmas cards dwindled, although recently they'd received emails and a photo of daughter Juno and her fiancé, which Simon had hidden somewhere, although he said he hadn't.

He'd surprised her by saying they had to go to the nuptials. He'd always been very careful with money, not exactly mean. Sometimes she wondered where his salary went – he was a lawyer after all. So she was taken aback by his plans for their trip to Australia. Think of it as an early silver wedding celebration he'd said, silencing her objections.

Beverley felt the front of her cardigan. All the silver buttons were in place and so perhaps it was something that had fallen out of the pocket.

She couldn't help it, she had to speak again and risk

Simon's annoyance. 'I've always thought Philippa fancied you. She never came to our wedding, do you remember?'

'I haven't got dementia. Of course, I remember.'

'Odd, wasn't it?'

'Not really. Australia is the other side of the world.'

The train trundled on and it would be impossible to halt it and ask them to let her off so she could go back to retrieve whatever had fallen over the side.

Now they were looking at a fish-cat (not catfish, she reminded herself), an animal which strolled lethargically around an artificial stream, dipping a paw in for its prey. In a different place, an aquarium, or on The Great Barrier Reef, that prey might be protected, something to admire. In this setting, fish were just food.

'I think it was all the cakes. You loved them, you used to wolf them down after lectures. I've never been able to bake cakes.'

'I'd eat anything that tasted good in those days, always hungry,' he agreed. She could hear the smile in his voice as he recalled his youthful days.

She remembered Philly's hand smoothing Simon's shoulder-length locks, and the way she said, 'Si, tuck in, have another slice, go on.'

What did it matter? It was twenty-five years ago. Now Philly's daughter, Juno, was going to tie the knot and would no doubt have the most delicious homemade wedding-cake imaginable.

Although cake wasn't something any of them would need in forty degrees and under a sweltering sun.

'How old is Juno?' she asked, although she knew perfectly well and Simon didn't reply. 'Getting married is so traditional – hardly anyone does it nowadays.'

Philly hadn't been traditional. The bloke she'd gone off

with was a casual boyfriend, a little older than her, he was a lecturer over on an exchange year. She'd bought her ticket to Oz and gone back with him as an adventure. It was probably just her way of getting out of any more medieval history exams.

Then she remembered. She took a sudden gulp of warm, tropical air. She felt a hot rush of anxiety, then terror, as she clasped her ring finger. The diamond and sapphire ring that Simon had given her last week for their anniversary had gone. That must be what had dropped off. It was quite loose and needed altering but there hadn't been time before they set off on their trip. She wasn't used to wearing it yet.

When they'd arrived at their hotel, Simon had said, 'Put it in the safe.' But she hadn't. She didn't completely trust hotel safes. She wanted this ring to sparkle on her finger at Juno's wedding and she hadn't wanted to take it off.

She'd long ago lost her cheap engagement ring and, at last, he'd given her a replacement.

It was another thing she would have to apologise for. He'd never, ever let her forget. She didn't know what to do.

Simon was still munching peanuts and dropping them over the side which she could hear was irritating people in the next carriage.

'You have an obsession with Philippa, Juno and their life,' he said. 'Try and relax. It'll be fine.'

What on earth did he mean? Why would she be obsessed with somebody she hadn't seen for decades and whose daughter she'd never met?

She felt in her pockets, around the hem of the cardigan, ran her hands along the seat but no. The ring had gone. She'd heard its faint clink as it bounced on the side of the carriage.

They were nearly at the end of their ride round the zoo. She could see café lights and the next queue of people waiting to board their train.

'It's the ring. Simon. The ring slipped off my finger and is lying back there by the track. I'm terribly sorry.'

'What? I told you to put it away securely, Beverley! Why didn't you do that?'

She hesitated, then she had to say again, 'I'm sorry.'

She'd had enough of being made to feel in the wrong over everything. If he'd bothered to find out her finger size before buying the ring, it would have fitted better.

If they tried to explain to their guide, she would pass them on to another official who might send someone down the line to find it and they'd be messing about for half the night and might miss the coach back to their hotel. They could miss their flight to Australia. More likely, no one would want to go out and search as the officials were unfriendly and uninterested in tourists. Or, if they did go, would they really return the ring to her or would they keep it and pretend it was lost? It would actually be easier just to reach an arm out of the train and pick up the ring themselves. They could try.

Simon sighed. 'We'll have to leave it. We can't wait.'

She was shocked he wasn't more worried. He hated wasting money. 'Leave it? But it's a valuable ring! Sapphires, you said. We can't afford to do that.'

'It is a shame you've lost it.' He hesitated. 'I'll get you another. We could claim on insurance.'

'You made a big thing about giving me that ring, and I want it back,' Beverley said. If it wasn't worth much then she was going to make him own up. In any case, she wanted to wear it at Juno's wedding. 'We'll do the circuit again. It will still be there.'

'We'll go round again then if we must,' Simon said sulkily.

Beverley was pretty sure she knew exactly where she'd dropped it – just beyond the hippos so that would be the patch populated by hyenas or jackals. So round they went, looking again at the shadowy shapes barely visible now the night sky had clouded over.

'Here we are,' Beverley said as they approached the hyena enclosure. As she prepared to reach down to the track, she peered over the side of the train.

Luckily, the train went very slowly to enable animal-viewing. 'There it is!' she cried, seeing something sparkling brilliantly by the track, perched on the edge of the ditch. It was lucky they were going so slowly. Simon switched on his mobile light, which made the guard call out a warning.

'I think I can—' She leant over, stretching her arm out ready to scoop up the ring.

'You'll never do it, short arms,' he said. 'Take the phone!' Simon threw the top half of his body over the side of the carriage, reaching out. At least he was tall which gave him more of a chance. But he reached too enthusiastically, too far. Losing his balance, he toppled over the side.

'Mind your head!' Beverly shrieked as he fell, then rolled, into the grassy ditch.

Two hyenas galloped over, their long snouts lifted, smelling his scent, their yellow eyes glinting. She heard his new shirt rip. 'Stop! Stop the bloody train!' she screamed as other passengers stood up, which they'd been warned not to do, and took pictures of her husband being mauled by jackals or hyenas. She didn't know which, but they seemed ravenous.

Moving the Statue

Alice could just make out some movement, sort of dusty smudges, fluttering round the old statue in the middle of the lawn. The statue was a child dressed in draping garments and holding up a rimmed plate which birds liked to splash about in or peck at crumbs on.

She would love to know exactly what birds they were. And how many. Finches or tits or some more unusual species. Now if they were nuthatches with their sleek blue-grey backs and habit of going everywhere in pairs. If the nuthatches returned, she would consider that a good omen.

Even though she got up from her armchair and walked, with difficulty, to the window she still couldn't decide what sort of birds they were. She had trouble with her vision; one of her eyes was worse than the other but she'd decided not to have the operation. Not after that last visit to the hospital.

No, what she needed to do was move the stone statue and one day soon, when she had the energy and when her legs obeyed commands, she would do this.

Then, suddenly, the birds had gone. Flown either into Frank's garden next door or further down the road to the couple, but they had a cat so she hoped not.

Come to think of it, she'd ask Frank to help her. You could ask Frank anything and if he had time, he'd do it. He was always dashing about, frazzled, wearing clothes that had a frayed or slightly shrunk look. Shetland jumpers you could see his shirt through. Trousers that didn't quite reach his shoes. You could see he didn't have a wife. She was sure, though, that this was half-term week, and he was a teacher, so he'd said he'd come in and do a few things for her.

Only a year or two ago she'd have shifted the statue herself without a second thought. Rolled it along on its base to the required spot just in front of her living room window, so she could watch the birds.

But if today was Tuesday, and she thought it probably was, then she had a feeling she'd arranged something else for the morning. Alice looked at herself, at what she was wearing. Her smart plum two-piece. She'd even squeezed her feet into her best shoes and for the life of her, she couldn't remember why. She patted her head – she had put her hair into a bun, with combs on either side.

That was the trouble with being old. Or one of the troubles. That was why lots of half-finished letters to friends or folded notes to herself perched on every table and chair arm, rather like birds. She was trying to tame her memory. She wandered around the room, picking them up and trying to decipher her own large, looped handwriting: 'Milkman please leave…' 'Dr 5.15…' 'Jane coming Tuesday at…' 'Shopping – sprouts (small), bananas 2 (ripe)…' 'Frank…'

Another trouble with being old was the thought that you weren't really doing anything, you were just keeping going. Not influencing life. Not moving statues. Alice had always been a great doer.

Once, eighty years ago, she'd skipped along Striding Edge. Once, she'd skated across a lake with her sister and eaten chestnuts from a brazier right in the centre. Now, what year would that be?

Once, her sister had come home (she could remember exactly what she looked like – green wool coat, fur collar, auburn hair waving to her shoulders) and she was still on the doorstep when she'd asked, 'What do you think, Lal, shall I say yes?'

Alice had said, 'Oh, he's a good man, Sis, you'll be happy with him.' And she had been, though they'd not had children and both were now dead.

Alice went into the kitchen to make two slices of toast. It was late – getting up had taken longer than usual. But why worry about mealtimes? She could please herself, couldn't she?

It was while she was laying the trolley to take into the other room that she remembered. The girl from Social... Security? No, Services...one or the other, was coming. The girl's name was Jane. Last time, Jane had come just before eleven, so she had a good half-hour until then.

As she ate her breakfast Alice recalled their previous conversation. To begin with, Jane had sat on the sofa and talked. Something about her father and his business, her mother who was depressed and her brother who was in trouble. Why had Jane told her all this? Haven't you got a boyfriend, she'd enquired? But no, Jane hadn't. She had her job and her hobbies. Knitting was one of them. Could that be right?

Then they'd had a cup of coffee. That was when Alice had started having misgivings. It was the way Jane watched her, the way she looked at her walking stick, the heavy kettle, the stiff tap that took a few moments to turn on and off. As if she was mentally ticking (or crossing) a list. Then Alice hadn't been able to find the coffee. Jane had started poking around the shelves, then asked, 'Is this it, Alice?' and laughed. Alice had put the coffee in an enamel canister marked Tea. Well, she didn't drink tea now – couldn't be bothered with bags or pots.

She was probably all right. A pretty girl with short curly brown hair and an earnest way of pursing her lips. No make-up, just neat little silver blobs in each ear. When she'd run out of space, she'd gone on to her nose.

Alice had put coffee cups for two on the trolley. She'd wait till Jane arrived to have hers. Didn't want to be stuck in the lav when the doorbell rang.

The whole thing had only started because of all that muddle with her pension book. All the phone calls and letters she'd written explaining things. Then someone she'd spoken to had said, 'I think somebody had better come round to see you.' Now, Jane was going to do an assessment. Or perhaps she'd already done it.

It was important that she didn't see anything which would make her say, 'Oh Alice, what's all this?' Like last time when she'd come and picked up a note from the hall table. 'Milkman? Posting letters?' Jane's voice had been disbelieving. But why else would she put out letters for him? And yes, she did leave the door unlocked on Thursday mornings: so he could collect his money, and post her letters. She couldn't walk to the box, could she? It was an arrangement. But Jane didn't like doors left unlocked.

She could only walk into the garden on good days. There were steps and a crazy-paving path that became slippery with rain or ice. But today was a bright, warm day with a breeze. She could manage to go out. But not before she'd checked the living room. Alice walked around slowly, picking up any notes she could see and putting them in the pocket of her wool jacket.

She had no intention of letting Jane find out about sleeping on the sofa, or sometimes just where she sat in the old Parker Knoll chair, wrapped in the patchwork quilt her sister had made while she was waiting to get married. One patch a week during her engagement. It was enormous.

Each patch was an individual. The dove-grey spotted muslin had been Mother's favourite blouse. Her sister had backed it with calico to make it thick enough for the quilt. The Madras cotton was a reminder of childhood teas. The red and cream fleur-de-lis print had been the curtains in the parlour, pulled over to keep the sun from the rug the day the officer came to tell Mother the bad news.

The curtains had remained drawn over for the rest of that year until they had to move house. She checked that she'd folded the quilt and hidden it behind the sofa. Then she sat down and looked out of the window.

If she had to, she would agree to the bleeper. She didn't want to have something hanging around her neck at all times, keeping an eye on her. But if it satisfied Jane, so that there were no more visits, then she'd agree to it.

But she would never agree to leave her own home. She'd rather die. Alice said this out loud again, to show she meant it. 'Yes, I would rather die.'

She would rather die than be herded into some old people's home. A place where Jane said meals were always at set times and they always gave you a choice (a choice between two things, neither of which she would like and which would come round regularly once a fortnight so you'd know which day it was because it was chicken marengo). A place where everyone had their own en-suite bathroom. Jane had looked at her pointedly when she said this. Alice knew that when your money ran low they made you share.

It was all right for some people, perhaps if they'd been used to having a husband or wife around and felt lonely.

Her independence had been hard won, not coming till she was forty-five and Mother died. You have the house, Sis had said, you deserve it. It was a small, terraced house but it was hers.

So then she'd found a job. She'd done various things. It was too late for a husband. When Alice visualised the only man she'd loved, handsome in grey-blue uniform, saying goodbye before going on his last flying expedition, she still felt a sharp ache.

She had friends. She was a single person, not an institution, and she wanted to stay that way.

She would sit down with Jane and encourage her to talk about her family. She'd show she could remember some of the details. She would agree to the bleeper. Then they would talk about other things. Alice would show her that she was still engaging with the world. She'd tell her about Frank. She would talk about the birds.

To do this she needed to see the statue, to see the birds flocking round, to name them. She'd show Jane the difference between a chaffinch and a bullfinch, between a blue-tit and a great-tit. It was years since she'd been able to see them clearly, but she probably knew a lot more about birds than Jane.

Alice gathered up the heap of crumbs from underneath the toaster and put them on a plate. She picked up her stick and made her way slowly down the back steps and into the garden. She placed the plate of crumbs on the outside window-sill. She walked diagonally across the lawn towards the statue. She wondered if the water-butt in the corner of the garden had its lid off again.

About a year ago she'd woken one night to hear a screeching sound and she'd come out with the torch to see what it was. A fox cub had fallen into the water butt and it was thrashing around, unable to keep its head above water.

She had heaved it out, a tremendous weight. Its fur was saturated, that was probably why. She'd dragged it over the lawn and lain it on the path, but it was dead. Frank had come over the next day to bury it for her. By then, its fur had turned dull and dirty, attracting flies. She didn't think she could do the same thing now. Her eyes were worse, her legs stiffer.

But she'd tell Jane the story – show that she wasn't afraid of being on her own at night.

Alice reached the statue and, leaning on her stick while she caught her breath, she stared at it. It was a while since she'd been close up to it like this. The stone had become pitted, the decorative details washed away.

As children they'd sat by it for hours, willing it to come alive, tracing their fingers over the carved snails, the frog and the smooth pebbles which had surrounded this child's bare feet. These things had gone. So, too, had much of the expression on its face. But she remembered the smile, the gaze turned upwards, the eyes wide with expectation.

Later, when she'd been stuck at home looking after Mother, she'd hated that mocking smile. She would have got rid of the statue but Mother wouldn't have anything changed.

Then it was too late and she'd just left it on the grass. She had accepted it. Started feeding the birds. Watching them.

With any luck, the nuthatches with their elegant long beaks would soon appear. They preferred a certain type of seed, picking it out of the mixed bird feed and leaving the rest. She'd ask Frank to buy her some.

Alice placed a hand around each of the child's arms and pulled. The statue wobbled slightly but its base remained firmly embedded in the turf. She knew she shouldn't be doing this. She should call over to Frank, he wouldn't mind. She could ask him to help her with... what was her name? The girl from the Social...?

In the distance, she heard a car door slam. She heard Frank's footsteps coming down his path towards their dividing fence. But she'd already heaved again at the statue.

She was quite a strong woman for her age. It was the bits of housework and gardening she kept going with.

All at once, one of her ankles turned in the too-tight best shoes. She fell sideways, pulling the stone statue over on top of her. As she fell, she had a brief, sparkling idea: Frank and the girl – they'd be well-suited, wouldn't they? But then the plate the stone child was holding thudded against her forehead. Some scraps of paper scattered from her pocket and were picked up by the breeze, which carried them randomly across the lawn.

Acknowledgements

Many people have helped me with my writing along the way and I would like to thank them all for their kindness and encouragement.

Thanks to Jamie McGarry of Valley Press for his support, to Lendal Press editors Seline Duzenli and Paige Henderson for their careful editing and enthusiasm, and to Peter Barnfather for text and cover design.

Thanks to Ian Burton, Della Galton, and Tracey Iceton for their insights and endorsements, much appreciated, and thanks to Chris Cuthbert and Carole Smith for their writerly companionship, and to everyone in Wimborne Writing Group for sharing writing and fun times over the years.

Thanks to Claire Keegan and Alba Arikha for their thought-provoking fiction courses.

I am grateful to Brisons Veor for allowing me a residency in Cornwall to think and write.

Special thanks to my husband, David, for his close reading of the stories and for his unstinting support.

About the Author

Sarah Barr was born in London, studied English at London University, has masters degrees in social sciences and creative writing from Southampton University, and now lives in Dorset where she writes fiction and poetry, leads writing groups, and works as a mentor. She has worked as a counsellor and as an Open University tutor of social sciences and creative writing. Her short stories have been published in anthologies, including in *The Cinnamon Review of Short Fiction*, *The Momaya Press Short Story Review* and *Wooing Mr Wickham* (Honno Modern Fiction), and in magazines including *The Yellow Room*, *Woman's Weekly*, *The Lady* and online with Fairlight Books. Her poetry pamphlet *January* was published in 2020.